The Tarot Card

by

jj Keller

The Tarot Card

Cover Art by *Kim Mendoza*

The Wild Rose Press
PO Box 708
Adams Basin, NY 14410-0708
Visit us at www.thewildrosepress.com
Publishing History
First Champagne Rose Edition, 2008
Print ISBN 1-60154-437-5

Published in the United States of America

DEDICATION

This book is dedicated to my friend,
Ramona Bauchert.

Chapter One

Stein Laxdale walked down the corridor reviewing his notes. He spun around to find the elevators. Damn, somehow he had gotten lost in the maze of *Yellow Fever*. Who named a hotel, *Yellow Fever*? Who would arrange a high-level meeting at a hotel called *Yellow Fever*? Kerry McClure, that's who.

Rune Technologies would not succeed without the deal with McClure Ventures. Everything he and Ian had worked for depended on this one business contract. So, if the man wanted to meet in a casino, then Stein would slide onto the chair beside him at the blackjack table. He'd meet him in the kitchen, if needed, to get the agreement signed.

He had to secure this deal.

A service elevator door swished open. He shoved the notes into the pocket of his swim trunk's, folded the shirt over his forearm, and dragged his body inside. He'd never get used to jet lag. He punched the dim yellow button, and took a step back as he ran a hand through his hair. He had to get some normalcy in his life.

"Stop," a woman's voice said, as a small hand pressed against his back.

He turned and took a pace back. A gypsy stood before him, a *sexy gypsy* wearing a long flowing

1

orange and gold skirt, with a white off-the-shoulder blouse and no bra. He had to look, it was Vegas after all and he was a man in need of creature comforts. He guessed her to be about five-foot-six with breasts that didn't appear to be silicone-enhanced. They were full, smooth and pliable. They rose and fell as she breathed, pushing against the tiny bit of supportive elastic of the see-through blouse.

He raised his gaze, her head remained bowed. She smelled like an exotic flower. He placed two fingers under her chin and lifted her face. She pulled back. *Startled from his touch?* In the next blink, her eyes softened. When he dropped his hand to hang limp at his side, her stance relaxed. Magnificent dark brown eyes stood out on her beautiful, delicate face. The gold scarf wrapped around her head hid most of her light brown hair, but added a glint to her eyes. She shifted from foot to foot as she straightened her blouse and tightened the belted scarf around her tiny waist.

"I'm sorry... Magda?" He nodded toward her name badge.

She shoved her blouse up onto her shoulders, closing off the gap which had allowed him full view of her breasts. "Quite all right. You didn't see me."

Kerry didn't correct him. Her name badge sported Magda because she would perform as a gypsy in the Magda tent for the library fundraiser. She ran her glance from his eyes to his bare chest to his tight swim trunks, keeping her gaze there a little too long. "Are you with the Chippendales?"

She clamped her teeth on her quivering lip to hold the nervous laughter inside. Goodness, he was gorgeous. His swim trunks weren't the typical boxer style, but tight fitting, with bulging pockets. Bits of white paper peeked out of one and the imprint of a cell phone outlined the other.

"No." He unfolded his shirt and slid it over his

head just as the elevator jerked to a stop.

She crashed into him and grabbed at his waist with both hands. He'd pushed his arms through the sleeves, but the cloth hadn't dropped into place before her fingers slid over the heat of his stomach. The cords of his slim waist and muscular stomach made her want to explore. Her heart pounded against her ribcage. *Chart the unknown.*

The main lights flickered off, leaving only the safety lights on the two sides. She yanked her hands away, and his shirt dropped into place as he stepped back. Could he be embarrassed about her touching him?

"Damn."

"I couldn't agree with you more," she whispered.

He pressed the emergency button. Part of her wanted the elevator to grind and moan into movement and the other part of her—the wicked one—hoped it would remain stagnant for a little longer. Perhaps she could get to know him and have a nice romantic interlude. She needed a bit of stress relief after the last six months of dealing with bureaucrats and her conniving uncle who wanted to take the CEO position away from her.

If she were to judge by her elevator companion's heated gaze, he found her appealing. He'd focused on her breasts long enough. She shifted, uncomfortable without a bra. It had broken a few minutes earlier, the front closure couldn't be repaired so she'd dumped it in the ladies room. On her way to the hotel room to get a new one opportunity for recreation had presented itself in the form of a Chippendale look-alike. Could she bring herself to take advantage of this man? *A brief interlude with a stranger in a stalled hotel elevator?*

"We're aware of the malfunction," a high pitched squeal bellowed from the tiny speaker. "We'll have it fixed in a moment."

"I guess we should just wait, and they'll get us out," she said, hopeful he'd make the next move.

"I'm sure they will," he responded.

The soft lights added a mysterious background. The man had to be over six foot with pale eyes. There wasn't enough time, before the bright lights went out to determine their exact color.

He ran his hand across his short-cropped white-blond hair. A firm chest existed below his polo shirt. She knew of his strength because her thinly veiled breasts had been snug against his wide upper trunk for a brief moment. They continued to tingle and peak from the contact with his tight muscular wall.

"Are you with—" His deep voice sounded loud in the small space.

"I'm with the library..." she said speaking at the same time, "You first."

"You're with the library fundraising event?" He leaned against the handrail, arms crossed, feet firm and steady.

Self-conscious about her appearance she hoisted her bag onto her shoulder. She crossed her arms, replicating his stance, and nodded.

"When I checked in at the desk, I noticed a flyer with a gypsy on the front. Now, it seems as though the gypsy has jumped off the page and I'm lucky enough to share an elevator with her."

"Now I feel awkward." She pulled her handbag in front of her.

"I'm sorry. I don't know why my thoughts are coming out of my mouth before filtering through my brain first." He scrubbed his hand through his short, spiky hair.

The elevator jerked, and he grabbed her arm. "Hold onto me, I'll keep you safe."

Her glance locked with his, and she smiled. He seemed harmless and wanted to protect her. Her heart raced as fast as the click-click of the elevator gears grinding above them. She'd like to touch him again. Maybe kiss those almost perfect-shaped lips. She didn't trust thin-lipped men. His faultless lips had the same full shape on top as the bottom. A deep ridge in the middle kept them from being perfect.

Rude, staring is rude. But, she could not stop herself, he was good-looking. It was difficult for her to keep her gaze off him. Strange, she hadn't had any interest in men for several years. However, the way his gaze discreetly traveled down, pausing briefly on her unbound breasts, made her think about her body. As a runner she was proud of how tight her muscles were, how agile she could be, but she'd never considered her form beautiful. Until now, as a result of how his breathing deepened, his fingers curled into her skin, and his blue eyes transformed into liquid heat.

She fit her hips against his side as he continued to hold onto her arm. Did he find her to be sexy? Was she sexy? Should she test her appeal with this man? She glanced up to meet his gaze.

Stein met her stare, her brown eyes searching his. She had a soft, untouched quality, despite appearing to be in her mid-twenties. His stomach muscles clenched. What the blazes was wrong with him? He rubbed his sweaty hand on the edge of his shirt.

"Are you on vacation?" Her sultry voice coiled through the dark interior.

"A little business and holiday, really," he said.

She pushed the ties of her head scarf behind her shoulder. The orange-gold color matched the cloth tied around her waist, which she twisted it around her palm. She released the tie and rubbed her index finger across the peachy orange of her nail polish on her thumb. Black ballet slippers peeked out from underneath her long skirt.

Say something. Her continued stare made him

restless. *Too much silence.* He glanced at her.

"*Yellow Fever* had a high scoring poker game last night. The winner walked away with half a million dollars...if you gamble." She gazed into his eyes and then lowered her glance to the floor of the elevator. Was she shy? Librarian quiet and introverted?

"I don't like to gamble with my money, but I'll be sure to toss the arm of the bandit."

She chuckled. "I think the phrase is, to pull the one-armed bandit."

"Ah, now you know how much I gamble." He kept his tone modulated, forcing the words to come out in a precise diction. His goal was to fit into the American culture and start-up a new market.

She looked up again. "Typically, I don't either, but after hearing the half-million dollar story, I must admit I did go into the casino and play some blackjack."

Her eyes glimmered with joy. Almost as if she was revealing a scandalous secret to him and only him. The intimacy was unquestionable. Should he act on the obvious attraction?

"Did you win?" He lowered his hand from her arm and squeezed her fingers.

"No, lost one hundred dollars in twenty minutes. I can see why there's a Gambler's Anonymous because it's tempting to try again—just one more time. I'll get it the next round sort of thing." She chuckled again.

Her laugh was sweet, a deep-throated feminine sound. More mature than a teenager's giggle, but not a harsh outright guffaw like an older woman might have. Stein thought she was a delightful package of contradictions, shy one moment and flirtatious the next. He considered asking her if she'd like to gamble with him later that night.

"We're having a problem with the controls," said

the voice from the black box. "We're working on it. We'll have you out as soon as possible."

He released her hand and checked his phone. Eighteen minutes without movement had quickly passed. Stein shoved his phone back into his pocket. He admired her ability to remain calm, he was sure his ex-partner would be climbing the walls by now.

The elevator bounced and dropped like an amusement park ride, fast and hard. She jumped closer to his side. He enfolded her into an embrace with one arm and held the rail along the sidewall with the other. The lights flickered on and off. He felt her heartbeat accelerate. She had to be afraid, alone with a stranger in a plummeting elevator.

The damn thing stopped. He braced his legs in the corner, allowing her legs to slip between his. He grabbed her around the waist to prevent her from falling. The security lights went off and they were immersed in total darkness. Her handbag fell to the carpeted surface with a thud as she rested securely in his embrace. He dragged her snugly against him, wedging them tightly into the corner.

"You don't have a crystal ball in your enormous bag to call forth the light do you?"

Her breath wisped across his face as she tittered. He released the rail and moved his hand to the side of her face. Her bandana had slipped and exposed her delicate ear. Stein leaned down.

"I like your laugh." He stroked his fingers down to the side of her neck.

She turned and their lips touched. A mere space of time and his mouth wanted to explore, devour hers. Her tongue reached out to lick her pink rim and touched his in the process. Of their own accord his lips pressed firmly to hers. At first she didn't respond. She held her mouth steady, and then he felt the movement. His heart beat a constant thump as she capitulated and leaned into him, giving into the odd desire rising between them, two strangers alone in a dark elevator.

Her shivers struck his inner core and he backed away. "What if I check to see where we've stopped? Maybe we're at a floor and the doors are stuck?"

"Great idea!" She sounded relieved.

He pried the gateway open, slowly, allowing light to enter. His muscles bunched and cramped, but his efforts paid off as he exposed a two-foot wide opening with about six inches below the floor. Stein couldn't get through, but the tiny gypsy could.

"I won't fit. Do you want to try?" Stein asked.

"Yes."

"Don't sound so relieved," he whispered.

"I didn't know it until now, but I don't like tight, semi-dark spaces," she retorted.

He chuckled, appreciating her honesty and sense of adventure. "Toss your bag up, and then I'll hoist you." How would her soft breasts feel underneath his hands? Would he smell her woman scent and touch her soft inner thigh as he helped her through the portal?

"What if it starts to drop again, I'll be clipped in half." She bit her lip.

"I'll hold you and feed you through. If any movement occurs, I'll pull you back."

"All right." She grabbed her bag, zipped it, and threw it through the opening.

"Face up, so you'll sit and swing through or face down and pull yourself through? Which is easier for you?" he asked.

Magda turned and placed her hands on his shoulders. She moved her hands back and forth sending twinges of desire into his stomach. Her pink tongue came out and licked her lips. She raised her glance to meet his. How could he possibly touch her body without his cock exploding out of his swim trunks?

"You've beautiful blue eyes. I think I have a plant at home, a variegated violet about the same color," she said.

His breath came out in short pants as he tried to keep her at a distance, resisting the urge to pull her snug against his fully erect penis, tight and firm.

"Personally, I'd rather you be face up." He tried to keep the raspy got-to-have-sex-with-you tone out of his voice, but she flinched and stepped back a space. Damn, he'd scared her. He needed to work on his charisma and most certainly his approach.

Had he lost his touch with women or had his last relationship with Maeve damaged him? How long did it take to recover from being used by a woman? Maeve was the reason he was in Vegas practically giving away his services to Kerry McClure. Maeve wormed her way into his bed, but he'd let her into his heart. She grabbed it, a portion of his company, and ran. Now he had to buy her out or sell.

"Face down," she said as she sighed. Sliding her hands down along his arms, she turned toward the opening. "I think it'd be easier for me to pull myself through the small opening and see where I'm going."

Stein grabbed her waist and lifted her to the exit. Her shaking hands slapped on the hotel floor, as she walked them forward. He breathed deep as he dragged his fingers from her slim waist to her shapely butt and muscular thighs. The sound of rending cloth tore through the air.

"I'm stuck," she shouted.

"Is it the shawl wrapped around your waist or..."

"What's wrong with your voice? I can't hear you. Talk to me!" Her voice held hints of fear or anger. He wasn't sure which. Christ, he needed to get control. He wasn't a bleeding teenager.

"Is it your shawl?" he choked out.

"I don't know, getting scared though. I heard grinding noises above, loud frightful scrapes and pulverizing."

The panic in her voice made him sweat. When she twisted around, he could see fear in her brown eyes.

Get over it, Stein, she's beautiful, she wants you, you want her, but this certainly isn't the time or place to do the staring game or soft touches.

"I did too, you want to go forward or back?"

"All but my legs are through, I want to finish."

"Ok. I'm going to put them against me and tug at the cloth."

"Hurry."

He moved her legs to his side, her light weight made her easy to hold with one arm. Reaching to her waistband, he snapped the shawl. It fell free and floated to his side. He dropped it onto the carpeted floor.

"It's not the shawl. If I pull your skirt it could rip." The wheels of the elevator made groaning noises.

"So do it!" she hissed.

Stein tugged her skirt at the waist, it pulled, but the material was quality. It didn't rip. "I'll need to move your legs, so I can use both hands."

"Fine. Whatever. Just get me free!"

He placed her legs on each side of his head, inhaling her musky scent with the movement. His cock pulsed in its upright position. The cords squealed, sparks flew, and the elevator shifted to the right.

"Hurry!"

The eerie clunking and loud clanging of wheels and wires sounded louder. The lift dropped a few inches. She screamed.

Stein grabbed both sides of her skirt and pulled. The material wrapped at her ankles and slid onto his hands. Her panties were pure silk, white, and high cut. The fresh clean scent of her skin wafted through the air as he slid his hands over her thighs, down her calves jerking the skirt along the way. He lifted one of her legs, and then the other. The cloth fell into his hand, and she was free.

She scurried through the opening, and reached back. He shoved her skirt through and wiped the sweat off his brow with the edge of his polo.

Her face appeared in the opening. "I'll go tell Krista at the desk you're still in there."

"Sure," he murmured.

Stein heard the pitter-patter of her ballet slippers on the marble floor. He picked up her shawl and noticed the white envelope. No writing was on the outside, and it hadn't been sealed. With a flip of the seal it opened. He slid out a note card.

Not a note card, a tarot card—The Hanged Man. Literally, a man hanged upside down from a branch with one leg crossed over the other. A self-portrait?

Chapter Two

Kerry walked out of the bedroom and meandered to the windows to enjoy the panoramic view of the mountains. The mist rose higher, almost reaching the white caps. She lifted her name badge off the counter, "Magda", and instantly thought about the incident in the elevator. The hotel clerk claimed a rescue squad would assist the man. She hoped he was able to get out. He'd touched her as no other man had. He'd inhaled as if he couldn't catch his breath and his voice had sputtered and cracked.

Goodness, what if he had a heart condition and she'd forced him to shove her through a small opening. She turned, took a few steps toward the bedroom, smoothing and drying strands of hair with the towel. She dialed the desk.

"Front desk, Tim, how may I help you."

"I'm checking on a man stuck in the service elevator. Did he get out?"

"Yes, miss. He's been released," Tim replied.

"Thank you." She disconnected.

Jessica came bustling through the door. "Hey, what happened? You said you were going to replace the broken bra and be right back." Her friend and co-worker made a straight-line to the mini-fridge and grabbed a juice.

"Got stuck in the elevator. Had to climb out through an opening the size of a peephole and lost my skirt as a Chippendale look-alike held my legs on each side of his head." Kerry pivoted and picked up her glass of iced tea, flecks of ice floated around the top.

Jessica coughed and spit the orange juice out her nose. Kerry handed her a pure white towel the same color as his hair.

"In the service elevator? Who was the guy?" she uttered between guffaws.

"You've some juice pulp on your eyebrow, the orange looks like a biodot. Yes, in the service elevator, so much for avoiding people. I don't know who he was, but he made my heart beat as fast as when I put the treadmill on ten. " Kerry set her glass on the bar and grabbed a piece of lemon from a bowl. The tang of citrus greeted her nose as she squeezed the fruit into the tumbler.

"No way." Jessica wiped the orange off her eyebrow and shoved her blonde bangs to the side.

"Oh, yes, he was tall, about six-foot, maybe six-two. White-blond hair clipped close to his head and a sloped nose with a tiny little dimple under his lip. It could be a scar, but it looked like a tiny crevice. He turned his gaze toward me, and I fell onto his broad chest. Touched his slim waist and tight, tight butt." Her fingers tingled with the memory and quivers went through her body. "He's the type of man who focuses on the key component of a woman's body."

Jessica raised a perfectly manicured brow, with a question flittering across her face.

Kerry raised two fingers into a V and pointed at her face. "He focused on my eyes!"

"Right." Jessica's azure eyes glittered and danced with humor. "Did you get his name? Make a date for later?"

"No. Planned to give him a free pass to the Magda's fortunetelling tent, but then I got claustrophobic." In truth, she got scared, not of being in a small space, but frightened about wanting *that* man. She had never desired to touch a male as she had him. When he kissed her, or she kissed him, she wanted to experience more. Feel more. She wanted to take a leap of faith and enjoy the guy and his attributes.

"You don't have a problem being in cramped spaces."

"I know. I didn't think I had a problem either. Apparently I do." Kerry picked up her drink and sipped.

"So, the manly man helped you get out of the elevator. I'm not sure how the lost skirt happened. Unless that was before he helped you out." Jessica laughed, holding her hand to her flat stomach. The dark blue knit dress showed every curve on her body. A tiny bit of envy ran through Kerry.

"Funny. He was helping me slide through the opening when my skirt got caught on something. I heard the grinding of the pulleys and fear took over. I told him to remove it." His fingers had been soft, dry, and sturdy and her inner thighs had tingled as he touched her skin.

"You told a strange man trying to stuff you through a tiny hole to remove your skirt?" Jessica asked with a smirk.

"Don't judge, you weren't there. I was stuck. I heard the elevator move. He asked me if I wanted to reenter and I told him no. I wanted out."

"So you said, rip off my skirt, Mr. Chippendale?"

"How sad, that you're taking my painful experience and making it slapstick." In retrospect, Kerry thought it was funny, but she wasn't going to encourage her friend.

"I did tell him to just get it off." Setting her drink on the tabletop, she plopped down on the cream and white stripped sofa and folded her bare heels under her thighs. A small burst of laughter finally broke through. "Now I think it's funny and very embarrassing."

Kerry ran her fingers through her hair. "While

in the shower, I thought I'd try to contact him. Find out his name, offer him my thanks, but now, I'm flustered. Thank goodness I kept it mysterious and didn't tell him my true name or ask his."

"You didn't tell him your true name?" Jessica tapped an index finger on her chin.

"He saw my name badge, and I didn't correct him."

"Well, aren't you the little game player. I've learned one new thing about you today that I didn't know in the twenty years we've been friends." A wicked little gleam appeared in her eyes as she smiled.

Kerry considered letting the comment slide, but her curiosity was far stronger than her self-esteem.

"Learned only one?" She held out her hand, palm up. "I'll take the bait, which one?"

"You, Kerry McClure, are not immune to male charisma. You've fallen for a stranger, never thought I'd see it in my lifetime." Jessica waved her hand.

Kerry halted the instant retort.

"Validations," Jessica said. "One, you didn't tell him your true name. Two, you asked him to remove your skirt, it's more likely you'd rip the damn thing than let a stranger touch your person. Three, there is a glint in your eyes as you talk about him. He must have been very good-looking and down to earth or you wouldn't have given him the time of day. Next, although you think you've gone claustrophobic, we've been spelunking together, so I know if you can go two miles underground with limited light you *do not have* a fear of confined spaces. So, it confirms my theory you've fallen for a stranger."

Kerry's chest tightened, and her throat closed off. Her heart beat with a fast rhythm, similar to a dream response as she plummeted off a cliff in freefall to the bottom. Nowhere to go but down. Could Jessica be right? Had she connected with that man in the few minutes they were trapped in the elevator? Cripes, she didn't even get his name. He did have a slight accent there at the end, European, maybe UK. She'd have to try and remember what the dialect was. At the time she'd only craved escape from herself and her reckless thoughts.

Jessica shook her head. "You know, love isn't a bad thing. You haven't experienced that emotion yet, so you may not have recognized it. Anyway, we've two hours until we're scheduled for the mystic realm. Can I talk you out of making me tell fortunes tonight?"

"It's for a good cause, Jessica. They don't get as much in government funding as they have in the past. The library meant a lot to my mother, and I want to help it survive."

"The McClure Foundation has provided enough funds to support it."

"I love that you're the financial genius of our organization," Kerry shook out her hair, ran her fingers through it and rose from the sofa. "It's important to me, Jess."

"I know, so I'll tell fortunes to balding gamblers. To clarify, can I wear an evening gown with a shawl over it and a turban, which I can remove later?"

"Yes. Have plans?" Kerry picked up her glass and took it to the bar.

"Yep." Jessica drank her juice.

"Do you want to change times? You can work from six to eight, and I'll work eight to ten?" Kerry removed a wide-toothed comb out of her pocket and drew it through her tangled hair.

"No, you want time to review the materials before tomorrow."

"It's just so important to get this service up and running before the thirty days expire." Kerry slid the comb into her pocket, walked over to the desk, and extracted papers out of her portfolio.

"I hope you decide to go with them. I'm certainly tired of interviewing the different tech guys. Do you think any of them have perfect eyesight or wear anything other than plaid?"

Kerry chuckled. "We haven't seen any yet."

"If you get this deal arranged, do you think the board will appoint you as the CEO instead of your uncle? The bastard! I can't understand why you have to prove yourself anyway, you are your father's daughter."

"Because I'm only twenty-five, inexperienced, and naïve according to Uncle Mike. I hope it works out with Rune Technology, too. It'll be the start of an entire new level of trade. Plus, the markets will be wide open for The Garden Center." Kerry had to make The Garden Center a success. As a child she'd always gone with her mother to the shop. The people were friendly, the plants full of life. It was a serene, sacred place. Visiting the Center became her motivation to follow her first path.

"The Garden Center, your baby. According to the market study, the landscape design services will be the most popular. Especially since it's online."

"I can't help but be excited about the store's floral design and unique gift area. It's underused now," Kerry said and held her arms close to her waist. She needed a bit of positivism in her life.

"I agree. Hey, do you have any of the tarot cards left? I wanted to give one to a great looking guy I met in the lobby. His name is Ian, and he has the sexiest European voice I've ever heard. Irish I think."

"Ian Johnston?" Kerry walked over to search through her bag. She had one before the darn plastic connector on her bra broke.

"Can't remember his last name. Of all of the thousands of people in Vegas, why did you mention that specific name right off?" Jessica tossed the empty juice bottle into the recycle bag.

"Can't find a card. Because there's an Ian Johnston with Rune Technology. One and the same you think?" It clicked. Her hero in the elevator had an Irish accent, of course Las Vegas was an international hub, so there wasn't concrete evidence her mystery man was also with Rune Technology. She scoffed at the thought. Highly unlikely.

"I don't know," she winked, "but I'll find out later tonight."

"Just put a tie on your doorknob, so I know not to enter," Kerry said.

Jessica laughed as she walked toward the bathroom.

****

Stein cursed the fates that left him stranded in the elevator for another ten minutes. After his release, he'd rushed into the *Yellow Fever* conference center foyer, which was blessedly cool. The floors were a yellow and gray marbled tile and polished gold metal works of art decorated the walls. He glanced around at the scattered bizarre, eclectic décor. A statue of Athena, a Greek mythology legend, stood beside the American Indian princess, Pocahontas. The statues were detailed, graphic, and gigantic.

He accepted the apologies of the staff and hurried to the information desk. The flap, flap, flap of his sandals against the marble floor drew the clerk's attention.

"I need to find a woman."

Tim, according to his gold-plated name badge, raised his pale face and frowned. He rose from his red velvet chair and cleared his voice.

"Sir, we don't provide that type of service. I suggest you check the special brochures found on any street intersection." The echo of his effeminate voice rang through the lobby.

Stein noticed a few older ladies entering the hotel glancing at him. They glared. He scowled at the man who misinterpreted his request.

"No, I need to find the lass who lost this scarf and envelope." He showed the man the items. "There's nothing indicating her name, other than she had a name badge, Magda."

"The local library is hosting a costume ball, and I know they had a woman named Magda in the group. They're using the conference room, but it's closed at this time in order to finish the sound checks. If you want, leave the items with me, and I'll ask one of the organizers to find the woman who lost them." He shoved a hand toward the items.

"No, I'd rather find the lass myself." Stein pivoted and turned back. "What is the name of the room where they are having the ball?"

"*Star Gazer Conference Room.*" Tim handed Stein a flyer, resumed his seat, and sorted brochures into piles. Stein had been properly dismissed.

Star Gazer Conference Room. The flyer had a fortuneteller hovering over a crystal ball and in a clear font on a slick milky surface was written, *Friends of Las Vegas Library hosts, Find Your Fortune Costume Ball.*

Due to the elevator incident he had the precise location of the room, and he walked directly there. He reached out to open the door, locked.

Damn. He'd have to come back later.

He returned to the lobby and took one of the guest elevators to the tenth floor, where he stowed the scarf and envelope in his room. Twenty minutes later, he found his business partner, Ian Johnston, poolside with a lager. He tipped the rich dark beer and set it on the table beside him.

"What took you so long? I've been here for an hour." Ian removed his sunglasses and placed them on the table.

Stein kicked off his sandals and sat heavily on the lounge chair. He hoisted the mug of warm beer and drank half of it. "Got stuck in the lift among other things."

"Seriously?"

"Seriously. Fortunately for me, I wasn't alone." Stein removed his shirt, wadded it, and threw it over the end of the lounge.

"It wasn't with Tim, the desk clerk, was it?" Ian grinned, revealing blinding white teeth.

"No, a beautiful brunette, brown eyes and a rack that begged to be touched." Stein leaned back on the lounge and closed his eyes. It had been too long since he'd been with a woman. It would be fortunate if he found someone, Magda, to hook-up with during his time in viva Vegas. He'd heard the expression, what goes on in Vegas stays in Vegas, and knew if he had a chance of breaking his six-month long celibacy, now was the time.

No, his priority had to remain with Rune Technology. He'd complete the transaction with Kerry McClure and then get rid of his partner. Damn Maeve and her greed.

A poolside waitress delivered a white towel. She smiled pointedly at Ian, who winked at her. The waitress didn't offer Stein any sexy, come-hither overtures. Disappointed, he grabbed his beer and took a deep thirst-quenching drink.

There was no accounting for taste. Stein glanced at his friend. Because of his insane ritual of running five miles each day, Ian was lean. He did have nice thick brown hair; whereas Stein had the Laxdale coarse white blond.

The waitress walked away and Stein replaced his drink on the table.

"I want to see Barry Manilow at the Hilton. I think I'll catch up with her and ask for directions," Ian said.

Stein frowned. "I'm not going to see Barry Manilow."

"You don't see him. You listen to his timeless music because it puts women in the mood for sex." Ian laughed. "Do you want to review the proposal for tomorrow?"

"Yes, but we've plenty of time. I need to find a little fortuneteller by the name of Magda, and convince her to spend some time with me on holiday. Do you want to go to a costume ball later?"

"In the Star-Gazer room?"

"Yes, how did you know?"

"I'll go because I've met a woman. Jessica. She has lovely blonde hair, sparkling blue eyes, and a dry sense of humor." Ian sighed. "She works at the fortuneteller booth at eight, apparently with Magda because she said to go to Magda's tent and she'd be there. I'm to hover until she finishes at ten."

"Great, unless they have a show together Magda will be finished at eight, and I'll ply her with my charm."

Ian snorted. "Right, you want to go at it."

"Don't you ol' man?"

"Right, but I know I will have sex, where you've only a thirty-seventy chance." Ian snickered.

"Such large odds, I'm usually seventy-thirty." Stein grinned and segued into the topic of business. "Speaking of odds, what do you think if we agreed to a year of free maintenance?"

"I think it's a smashing idea. We've the best equipment, so there won't be but a few odd occurrences." Ian situated the sunglasses on the bridge of his nose and settled into the comfort of the padded gold mesh lounge. "And from your sappy expression, you'll want to take all of the trouble calls, so you can return to the States," Ian muttered.

"How long have we known each other, Ian?"

"Since nappies. Why?"

"Have you ever known me to be so excited about a skirt?" Stein choked back a laugh, since the last time he touched her was to remove her skirt.

"You don't think the continents are going to be a problem for you?"

"I'll map out a solution." Stein slid the sunglasses onto his nose and contemplated how to approach the beautiful Magda. "What happened with the desk clerk you were going to pursue?"

"I was waylaid by the magnificent Jessica. Beautiful women at every turn in Vegas."

"You know, she's probably a snooty librarian, spouting facts like a talking encyclopedia." Stein lifted the mug again.

"She'll more than likely tell me to stuff it," Ian said.

"You do talk a lot." Stein sighed.

"Because you don't. There has to be a balance." Ian swung his legs over the side of the lounge. "Man, did you see that? She took her top off right in front of us, she's bare arse naked."

Stein removed his sunglasses, squinted to look over at the kidney shaped pool which sported a floating bar on one end. The woman Ian spoke of had lines on her face and sported a fresh scar near her left eye. She had been hardened by life.

"Sit back, rotter, we'll quickly review the strategy for tomorrow." Stein picked up his journal and jotted down notes.

"I'll just wander over to the bar and get some refills." Ian shot off the chair and hustled toward the bar and the not quite naked lady.

Chapter Three

Stein stood at the opening of the tent, waiting for Magda's current customer to finish, a teenager about the same age as his seventeen-year-old niece. He glanced behind him, there didn't appear to be a line of fortune-seekers, so he'd get a chance to talk with her after the teen was finished.

Magda's soothing voice came through the tent flap. "Your future will be filled with many adventures, and you'll find true love," she said.

He smelled the fortuneteller's perfume, the same scent she had on earlier in the elevator. A floral scent meant to tantalize men, and it worked because he craved her after a single whiff. The soft light within the tent gave her an ethereal luminescence.

The woman he had fantasized about all afternoon was dressed in a sleeveless black V-necked dress. When she flipped the gold shawl over her shoulder one of the large gold hoop earrings, rocked back and forth. She placed her hand to her ear to stop it. Instead of a turban, she wore a thin headband that had sequins sewed onto it. Knotted at the side of her head, two streamers dangled down the front of her dress. The pale pink color emphasized the delicate breasts he desired to touch.

"Thanks, Magda."

"You're welcome, Connie." The teen walked out of the booth, taking with her a pungent tobacco scent.

The ringing of a cell phone had Stein halting at

the entryway.

"Hello. No problem. I understand. It's been constant, but I'm tired of looking into the clear glass and seeing nothing but air. Memorizing the tarot cards helped. I sailed through those readings." She paused.

"Jessica, you've never had a problem with BS, so it doesn't matter that you didn't study-up for it. I've been performing on a wing and a prayer. I'll see you in twenty minutes." She closed the phone.

"Magda?"

"Yes, do you wish to have your fortune told?" She lowered her already sexy deep-throated voice and turned to look at him.

Her skin glowed with a rose tint. The woman twisted in her seat and pulled the wrap up closer to her neck. She fiddled with the cards resting in the center of the table and then moved the crystal ball to the edge. Why was she so nervous?

"I wanted to return these items to you." Stein held out the shawl and envelope.

"Thank you." She glanced briefly into his eyes and then extended her fingers, painted with a bright red polish, and took the scarf.

"The envelope has a tarot card inside, allowing you a free, soul-searching, cosmic reading. Do you wish to have the card read?" A shy smile left her lips, and she glanced down again. Maybe she was embarrassed about the elevator incident.

He wished to do more than have a reading with her. However, as a means to an end, why not? Stein sat down in the chair across from the beautiful and sexy Magda.

"Sure, what do I do?"

She lifted her head and flashed him a bright smile. The bangles at her wrist jangled as she waved her hand at him. He handed her the envelope.

"Ah, the Hanged Man—notice how he dangles

from a branch. This means you should suspend action, pause to reflect on what is important in life. Live in the moment." She affected an accent, actually very close to the true Romanian gypsies he had met in his travels.

"Do you mind if I ask if you are married?" She pierced him with a stare.

"No." He smiled. "You're the one who sees all. Tell me."

"No, you are not married, or no you do not mind my asking?" She deadpanned in return.

"No, I'm not married," he replied. "Does my marital status change the outcome?"

"Perhaps. The Hanged Man indicates it is time to let go, and give in to an emotional release. You should end a struggle. It will be difficult for you to give up control. However, change your mind and sacrifice if necessary. Your card directs you to go one step back, and two steps forward." She set the card to the side.

"Are you referring to my personal life?" He plucked the card from the table and slid it into his suit jacket pocket.

"I do not know, it has not been written in the cards."

"One step back and two steps forward sounds like a dance step. After you're finished with telling fortunes would you dance with me?" Stein reached out and touched her hand. The perfumed softness made him quickly imagine pulling her across the table and seating her on his lap. A dance would surely occur, and he would lead.

Magda turned her hand over in his, and their fingers entwined. She glanced up and a smile, as bright as the ballroom light, burst from her face.

"Are you available, Magda?" A blurry-eyed man swayed at the entrance, licking his fat lips with a bloated tongue.

"No, she's not," Stein snapped.

"I paid to get my fortune told by this little lady."
The man pointed a stubby finger at her.

Stein slid out of the upholstered chair and
swiveled. There was at least six inches in height
difference between them, and he knew the broadness
of his shoulders would intimidate the man. The
drunk lifted his glance and stepped back.

"Sorry, guess I had the wrong tent."

A pale woman with blonde hair entered the
enclosure, wearing a turban and tight fitting dark
blue dress on what appeared to be a perfect thirty-
six, twenty, thirty-two shaped body. She slid by the
man, as he pivoted to leave.

"Hi! What was that all about?"

"A drunk. Beware! If you have any problems call
my cell, and I'll bring security." Magda quickly
answered, her accent gone.

"No worries, Ian's going to hover around the
area until I'm done." She swung her baby blues at
Stein and held out her hand. "Hi! I'm Jessica
Watson."

"Good evening, I'm Stein Laxdale."

She shifted her glance to Magda.

"Well, THIS Magda's done. Have a nice time,
Jessica. I'll see you later." Kerry stuffed the scarf
into her oversized handbag and heard Jessica asking
Stein Laxdale about being part of Rune Technology
just as she slipped out through an opening at the
back of the tent.

She made her way to the exit, via the kitchen.
As a gambler's luck would have it, Ava Martinez, the
library foundation director, stopped her retreat
within inches of the door.

"Kerry, I have to tell you I'm so excited about
the event. So far, we've exceeded what we hoped to
get in funds. What a marvelous idea!" Ava grabbed
her arm and wouldn't let go. Her luck certainly

wasn't in the stars tonight.

Kerry looked behind her, hoping she had time to avoid the man who sent her heart beating as fast as the tambourine in the band. Lady Luck continued to spit on her, as the man in the elevator was Stein Laxdale, co-owner of Rune Technologies. Because of how they'd met, he would see her in a less than dignified way. How was she supposed to come to an agreement with him over the board room table tomorrow morning?

Her mouth felt dry. There wasn't enough water in all of Nevada to slake her thirst for Stein. For the first time in her life she wanted a fling, and the man she wanted it with was off limits.

Ava held on to her arm with a determined grasp. "Kerry, I want to introduce you to my son, Kevin." She reached out and pulled a short, stocky man forward. "Kevin, this is the lady I've been telling you about. Her mother and I were good friends."

His hair, the color of a raven's wing, was so shiny and black it matched his shoes. His dark brown eyes sparkled with mischief, as if he knew about his mother's scheming and didn't oppose it at all. A high forehead and rounded face made him a handsome man, but lately she found that she preferred chiseled cheeks and white-blond hair.

"Nice to meet you Mr. Martinez, I hope you're having a nice time at the event. I didn't see you at the fortuneteller's tent. Did you have your future forecasted?"

His cheeks took on a red hue. In all probability the man went to Delilah's tent. Good for him.

"Why don't you two dance? This is a lovely ballad, by Sting I think." Ava shoved them onto the dance floor.

On stage a petite dark-haired woman belted out "Fields of Gold", the Eva Cassady version. The soft melody, a little Irish in origin, made Kerry yearn for someone to tell her he wanted her to stay with him, to be his love. Blue eyes and a winsome smile flashed through her head. She shook the thought away. When had she become so scatterbrained?

"I'm not sorry about my mother's anxiousness to have us together because I find you to be a beautiful woman. If you want, we'll dance through this song. I'll entertain you. You throw your head back in laughter to make her think I'm good at this romancing thing. Then we'll see where the night leads us." Kevin's voice was dark and husky, much like the man himself. His downcast eyes made him appear shy, and she found it endearing.

"All right, Mr. Martinez—"

"Call me Kevin." He took her into his arms, placing one of her hands on his shoulder and one entwined with his. His other hand held her bag at her waist. A nice gesture. His hold on the purse prevented it from flapping against her side and subsequently falling.

"Kevin. Because I'm very fond of your mother, I'll dance this one dance. I'll smile and laugh. At the end of the song, I'll need to retire to prepare for a business meeting."

He had fluid dance steps and a saucy little rhythm to his hips. A quick turn and she made eye contact with her dream lover. Stein's eyes narrowed. She tore her gaze from his, unable to hold it.

"Maybe I can change your mind," Kevin whispered into her ear, and then touched his lips to the side of her mouth. The scent of peppermint flowed into her nostrils. She flung her head back and laughed.

"Good laugh, Kerry, very flattering," he said. "We'll dance through another song."

Not likely, as I plan to escape as soon as possible. The ballad seemed to go on and on. The words beautiful in their simplicity, and she continued to yearn. Her eyes searched the outer rim of the dance floor to find him. *Traitorous heart.*

She found him. Stein stood at the edge of the dance floor, talking to one of the Delilahs. Librarian-Madison. Although her shift had ended, she remained in costume and her stomach muscles were so taut they stood out in the dim lights. Unreasonable jealousy sparked through Kerry. Why would he be interested in Kerry with her wider hips and fatigued posture when a belly-dancer for the night, complete with diamond stud in her perfect little navel, stood right in front of him?

Kevin lifted her chin and spoke directly into her face. "Would you like to?"

"I'm sorry, my mind was on business." What was wrong with her, she tried to run away from Stein, yet, she couldn't keep her gaze off him.

"Ouch, not very flattering." Kevin pulled her close as he placed her hand under his suit jacket, and on his less than trim waist. "I asked if you would like to have a late dinner."

His free hand went to her left buttock. She reached down to shift his groping fingers to her waist.

"I'm sorry, the song's at an end, and I need to leave now. Thank you. You're a very good dancer." Kerry nodded toward Ava and made her way to the nearest exit.

The door handle felt cool beneath her hot fingertips. Freedom beckoned. The sense of flight ran strong through her veins, until his soft, lyrical voice flowed over her.

Warming her.

Making her vibrate in all the right places.

"What? You'll dance with Casanova, but not me? It looked like his nose took up residence in the middle of your uh...chest."

She lifted an eyebrow, it sounded as if he'd said

breasts. Surely he couldn't be so bold.

Kerry felt his breath on her neck. An instant flash of his holding her legs on his shoulders while he helped her flee went through her mind. She dropped her hand from the door handle and pivoted.

"Mr. Laxdale, I'm sorry, but I've an urgent need to ..."

"Escape?" He grinned, his smile playing havoc with her heart.

Her face flamed with heat. Yes, the getaway was foremost in her mind.

She'd only known him for a few hours, and a lifetime. His email transmissions were filed in a folder, so she could reread them whenever loneliness invaded. She referred to them often.

At first his correspondence had revolved around business, all proper and precise. Then he relaxed and told her about fishing, playing rugby with some of his friends, and hiking in Wales. She read between the lines. He unknowingly revealed his true self, the one she wanted to know intimately. The real, live man was so much better than the emails.

"Not at all. I've an appointment with a treadmill and if I don't get to the fitness center before midnight, we both lose." She placed her palm on the silver handle.

He grabbed her around the waist, swung her, and braced her against the wall. The door flung open and snapped against the frame. A waiter appeared from the other side, glasses jiggling on a tray.

Kerry looked into Stein's face. "Thank you. That would have put a damper on my workout."

His arms were on either side of her head, and his tall, powerful body pressed flush against hers. Liquid pooled at the junction of her thighs and her stomach muscles tingled. His lips touched her ear, sending a trace of electricity through her entire being. She inhaled his cologne, a mix of fresh outdoors, cinnamon, and spice.

"I'll give you a workout if you'll let me."

Her darn knees weakened at his whispered offer. She licked her lips and met his intense gaze.

Chapter Four

Kerry wanted to experience one night of relaxation, one night without fear of disappointing her uncle, the board members, or the people expecting her to bring their business out of the red. She wanted to simply be a woman, if only for one night.

"I'd love to dance," she murmured, while her heart fluttered like a flag in the wind.

He smiled, as if he knew she'd counter his offer with one of her own. She tucked her arm in his. His twinkling eyes and white-blond hair were so appealing she just couldn't resist.

"You're taller this evening." His glance met hers, close to the same level. Yes, she was taller tonight, and it was intentional. She'd hoped to have this encounter. She wanted him.

She lifted one of the black, open-toed designer shoes for him to see. "Heels—a solid three inches. I usually wear them, but had to stand on my feet for four hours earlier today, so I wore flats," she weakly responded. Cripes, she was babbling around this guy. Granted his face and form were perfect, regardless, *focus*.

"Do you want to talk about *earlier today*?" he asked.

"Not especially. I thank you for helping me get out of the elevator, but I'm still in the embarrassment mode." She tucked a piece of loose hair behind her ear.

"Then we'll save that conversation for another

day, and I'm sure we'll laugh." He smiled and wrapped his arm around her waist, guiding her through the mass of people.

"Would you like to get a drink, or go straight to the dance floor?"

A quick image of both of them naked on the floor of her hotel suite flashed through her mind. Soft music, Michael Bublé would be good, port wine, chocolate, and a roaring fire set inside a white columned fireplace. As a result of her little fantasy trip, her voice came out as Magda's, wispy and throaty at the same time. "A drink sounds good."

They navigated to the bar, decorated as a pyramid with fake beige and brown blocks. She slid onto a stool sporting a fig leaf on the backrest.

"What will you have?"

"A gin and tonic." Wine was too close to her fantasy. Stein leaned over to tell their order to the bartender. She glanced around to see how the others were doing. A line of patrons, primarily men, were in front of Cassandra's tent, and Delilah's pavilion had a large crowd of old, bald men standing around. The lights inside the white canvas created a shadow effect as Delilah performed her belly dance.

Stein turned around, so his front faced her and his side was to the crowd. The bartender placed a short glass in front of her, and a dark beer within reach of Stein.

"Tell me about your name, it's unusual," she said to Stein and lifted her drink to sip. The heady aroma of the alcohol, a twist of lime and mist of carbonation meant to suppress her fantasy, served to provoke her desire. The slight tickle from the fizz was a reminder of the soft hair at his nap. Would a taste of the beverage be her drive to go beyond reason?

"I am unique in many ways." He lifted and lowered his eyebrows.

Although the remark was cheesy, she found herself laughing. Drawn to this man not only because of his broad shoulders and sexy smile, but the way he tilted his head when he listened. He'd offered to help her escape that claustrophobic box and made the effort to return her scarf. He tracked her, despite the detour as luscious Madison plied her wiles.

When his glance roved over her face and continued its way down to her ankles, she was glad she made a special effort to add the gold ankle bracelet. The look in his eyes, as if he appreciated what he saw, caused her heart to throb, increasing her excitement. She wiped the condensation off the side of the glass to cool her hot hands.

If she was growing wet from a simple glance, what would happen when they danced later? Would his hands roam over her body? To glide in his arms, to touch her breasts against his chest filled her with anticipation. She lifted her drink for a sip and let her gaze dip lower. And she would encourage the roaming.

She wanted to experience the unknown and to take a walk on the dark side by having a one-night affair. He was her dream lover and obviously interested in her. Should she risk a liaison with a virtual stranger for one night? Could she?

But he wasn't a stranger.

She had been corresponding with the owner of Rune Technology, Stein Laxdale, for the past two months. Two weeks ago, Stein visited all of the mill sites in Indiana, Kentucky and Virginia accompanied by one of the members of her staff. Kerry had experienced his dry wit and his brilliant mind from the documentation of his findings.

Was it fair to tempt him, use his manliness to ease her sexual frustration without revealing her true identity?

Was it ethical?

Was it moral?

Kerry's emotions roiled through her. His appeal, strong and vibrant, was enough that she'd have sex with him if it came about naturally, but then she'd have to cancel the contract meeting. She could not have sex under false pretense and follow up with a business meeting. She didn't operate that way, neither in her business nor her personal life.

Then something else occurred to her. What if Jessica stood in as her proxy at the meeting tomorrow? The deal would work out, Rune Technology would get the business in the Midwest they craved and Stein had worked so hard for, and she would get her CEO appointment.

Stein continued sipping his drink and talking about the history of his name and ancestry. He was unaware of how fate could have worked in his favor. She had never been a possessive person, but she thought of him as hers. Kerry knew all of the information regarding his name, because she had asked in an email two months ago. But now, deciding to engage in an affair with him, she leaned in and listened to his voice as he shared his saga.

"So German based Stein or Stone is my first name and Norse originated Laxdale, which means salmon. Since, I'm from Ireland I have the accent tossed into the mix. You're not falling off the stool because of boredom, are you?"

She shook her head. She had slid to the side. Second thoughts made her want to leave. Not because of boredom, rather she desired him and it terrified her. Good thing she had read the email about his name and family history, at least five times, so she could ask intelligent questions. He'd slipped into his melodious Irish accent. She wanted to lean into him, have his soft words slide over her skin. *Calm down, Kerry, this is so unlike you.*

He touched the back of her hand, a slow caress.

"Ah, a lurching song, if you've finished your drink, let me impress you with my dancing skills." His words were stated so low only she could hear.

She entwined her hand with his and slid off the stool.

"What's a lurching song?" she asked.

"It's an up close kind of song used for slow dancing. A rhythm which allows two people to connect, lock hips." He grinned and the crevice under his lower lip disappeared. She wanted to run her tongue over it.

Kerry swallowed. She'd burrowed herself into a sexual fantasy and now needed to return to reality, before she moved hip to hip with him on the dance floor. A few minutes to get the thought out of her head would help.

"I'd love to. I need to put this bag in the tent." She picked up her large black leather satchel. Not expecting to stay at the event after her shift was over, nor expecting to dance, she hadn't exchanged her oversized handbag for an evening one.

He placed his hand low on her waist as they wove through the room. Arriving at the sultan's tent, she lifted the flap at the back of the pavilion and dropped her bag inside. Jessica held out an invisible tie from her neck and laughed. Kerry frowned and snapped shut the cloth opening. Had Stein noticed Jessica's antics? She hoped not, that would raise all sorts of questions.

The band was playing "Kissing a Fool" with a George Michael look-alike singing the lyrics on stage. Stein drew her close. She started to put her right hand into his, but he lifted her arm to rest on his shoulder. An instant memory of how her legs felt on his shoulders earlier sent an electric jolt down her spine.

Relax, it's just a dance. The George Michael

replica was very good, with his whiskey-hued voice. She inhaled. The sweet scent of Stein's sandalwood cologne wafted into her nostrils, reminding her of the closeness they shared in the elevator. Kerry exhaled, her breath blowing the hairs through the V opening of his shirt. His tie had been loosened and the top button unfastened.

"Tired?" he asked. "It's been an... eventful day for you."

"Not really tired. I'm relaxed." *And you feel so strong and sexy against my body.*

The song ended and the band went into "Crazy Little Thing Called Love" by Freddie Mercury. Dancers separated and swung about in time with the lively tune. A variety of eras were represented on the dance floor, some people hopped a fifties swing propelling their partner over the head; others seventy's disco, pushing the woman out and flicking her back like a rubber band; eighties and ninety's rocked their own version with no real pattern; and the younger set swayed and threw their arms into the air.

Stein continued to hold her close, with the same replicated, rhythmic motion as the slow song. She lowered her head to his shoulder. Her cheek pressed against the soft fabric of his black jacket. It smelled like him. Underneath the fragrance of the cologne, hovered another scent. His own, an aphrodisiac to her senses. Pure man.

"Could it be Magic" followed the fast love song, and she felt his hands slide from her waist to rest firm against her hips. He drew her snug against him. The contact of their full bodies, his maleness outlined and fitted against her stomach, caused her muscles to jump. A slow burn started in the vortex between her thighs. She remembered how lovely the sensation of being held and romanced, with skin touching skin.

"Who sings this song?" he whispered into her ear. The tiny hairs around her ear moved and tickled. A slow and steady tingle climbed from her upper thighs into her stomach. She clenched her muscles, pulling her vaginal lips together. It didn't ease the tremble that formed into an ache. Instead, her desire to experience fulfillment strengthened. She had to find that missing part to make her whole.

She lifted her head and the tip of her nose brushed the nape of his neck. "Barry Manilow, I believe."

"I guess you do have to listen," he murmured. A little shift and his lips would be in line with hers.

"What was that?"

"Would you like to go to my room to talk and order dinner?" He kissed her temple.

She closed her eyes in ecstasy and anticipation. If she said yes, it would happen. He would hold her in his arms and perform as the stallion depicted in the lyrics. Would she touch the sun?

He had danced them to a secluded area behind a cluster of artificial potted palms. Ten-foot-high, full, flat green branches hung over their heads. They were alone in their own little jungle. Wild thoughts ran through her head as the fever spiraled downward, deep into her belly.

She wrapped her arms around his neck and drew him down to her. He moved his arms, one surrounding her back and the other up her side, touching the lower part of her left breast. She shivered and leaned into his hand as he shifted his touch a little higher. Her areola peaked and pointed, begging for more. His kiss was soft, searching, and questioning. Tipping onto her toes, she pressed deeper into his embrace. She needed to know if they fit.

His tongue explored the contours of her mouth, and she tasted the beer he'd drunk earlier. Her tongue grazed his, and they played touch and caress.

They fit.

Kerry broke away, intending to experience a crazy little thing called love. "Stein—"

"I'd like to learn more about you, Magda."

Chapter Five

Under the palms, in the secluded corner of the conference room, Stein called her Magda. A blast of cold air surrounded her and the sweet ache between her thighs lessened.

"Stein," Kerry whispered and unclasped her hands from around his neck. "I can't do this. I'm sorry. Good-bye." Other than lowering her hands to his chest she didn't move.

"What?" He shook his head, a slow movement back and forth.

"I'm not who you think I am." She moved her chin out of the way for his lips to have easy access to skin.

"None of us are who we think we are. Let's talk philosophy later." He nibbled at her earlobe. His tongue flicked her dangling earring out of the way as he nuzzled her neck.

She had to halt his lovemaking before he went further. How could she stop him? His hands roamed from her waist up to her shoulder blades, his kisses finer than any communion she'd ever experienced. Low in the juncture of her thighs, that joyful ache returned. What was happening to her? When she'd had her sexual experience with Jimmy Hornpecker she never felt this way and she hadn't had any clothes on at the time.

She and Stein were fully dressed, albeit bound as tightly together as she knew two people could be in a room full of party-goers. Yet, she had the strongest desire to strip down and let his rough fingers touch her skin.

He was the mighty oak, strong and unrelenting, feet firmly planted on the ground and she was a poplar tree, decorative, talented, and needing pleasant surroundings. The poplar tree took its partnership with other trees very seriously. And so did Kerry.

"No," she whispered. The agony in her voice wasn't convincing to her, why should it persuade him?

She shook her head, placed the palms of her hands on his shoulders and nudged. His hands maneuvered down her back and tugged her as close as possible. She added a bit of force. He locked his lips on hers, and she took him in.

"Look out," someone shouted.

Out of the corner of her eye she saw a palm tree teeter as Stein jerked her to the side and placed his large powerful body in front of her as the tree fell. She peeked around his finely woven jacket to see a man wrestling with the trunk of one of the massive palm trees. The backside of the fallen fellow's shirt had a bright orange setting sun beach scene that appeared to be congruent with the branches.

Their sanctuary had been invaded.

"Sooo saary, man." The drunk's lips barely shifted.

Stein held out his hand to help the obviously drunk man. His eyes opened to reveal a glazed over look and his body movements were sluggish and inept. The intoxicated reveler took Stein's hand and rolled to a stand.

A security guard rushed forward. He held the communicator box at his shoulder ten-fouring while his other hand wound around an ominous looking black stick.

"I hate to state the obvious, but he's a happy drunk. I don't think you'll need to use the baton." Stein righted the sloshed man. The guard placed his weapon back in its holder.

"Thank you, sir. Sorry for the inconvenience." The well-built guard held onto the man's polyester sleeve, squishing the setting sun into an accordion shape as he hauled the partygoer away.

Moments later two men in gold uniforms righted the felled tree as Stein secured a hold on her hand and tugged her toward the exit.

"My purse."

He circumvented a table and went around the fortuneteller's tent. He reached in and grabbed her bag. Taking her hand in his again, he rushed them out of the conference room. They entered the guests' elevator, and he selected a button from the lit panel. She knew it wasn't her floor. He didn't know her name—ergo—he didn't know what floor to choose. The man certainly took a lot for granted.

He hadn't muttered, uttered, or grumbled one word. His thumb roamed over the palm of her hand in snail-like circular motions, making her aware of him physically. The scent of a freshly laundered linen shirt filtered through the air as he shifted his jacket aside to withdraw his room keycard.

The elevator doors swished open. He released her hand and wrapped his arm around her waist. The large handbag bounced at her side, and his fingers slid between her waist and the leather.

Let the inhibitions go, Kerry. Enjoy the moment. He doesn't know who you are. Live dangerously. Have a fling!

Stein didn't know her, but she knew him. She understood how important the business deal was. Oh, she recognized his success and the possibility of exceedingly long years of accomplishment. However, if he had the contract with her company he could buy out the rogue partner and not relinquish any of his financial base or clients. She had to end this or she, representing her company, couldn't hold the meeting tomorrow.

He opened the hotel room door and held it ajar. She had a choice to make. Seize all that she could from this erotic, romantic encounter, or bale.

Kerry McClure sashayed into the room.

Other than the blue and cream palette, the quarters matched hers. The large print over the bed presented statues of Greek Gods instead of a field of flowers. The window drapes were open, casting multi-colored lights onto the bed and supple overstuffed chairs near the window. A green light flashed on the telephone indicating he had a message. The soft whoosh of the door closing caused her heart to palpitate as fast as the blinking light.

Stein's hands rested on her shoulders, his sandalwood scent tantalizing her. She leaned into him and her handbag slid down the bare skin of her arm, taking with it her shawl. She caught it with her fingers. He took the bag and shawl and threw them.

Kerry inhaled a deep soul-searching breath. The words formed, but were shut-out when his mouth ravished hers. She tucked her arms behind his neck and pressed her aching breasts against him. *Oh, this feels so right. We fit so well together.*

His lips moved down to her neck. She shoved his jacket off his shoulders, and he shook his arms until it fell quietly to the floor. The tie had to go. She tried to unknot it, but it tightened instead of loosened. He lowered her hands to rest flat on his firm chest. With a flip of his fingers the knot fell away and the tie hung along the sides of his button-down. The silk caressed her fingers as she drew it painstakingly down his muscled chest.

He inhaled. She glanced up at him. He had that look on his face, the one she had witnessed earlier, like he was tired or sated or excited. She couldn't define the expression, but it made the ache between her thighs stronger, the muscles vibrated within.

Without losing eye contact, she slid the button through the hole. His breathing came in quick little pants. Oh, the power a woman could hold and eke out as she wanted. Dragging her hand along his waist, her fingers unbuttoned a pearl disk.

"Please," he hissed.

Please what, she wondered? He still panted those tiny little breaths. At one time he must have popped a mint into his mouth because the scent of peppermint came out with each puff of air. She raised her face, but her eyelids remained heavy, resting half-way instead of closing. Her lips were dry, so she rolled her tongue over them, while she continued to unbutton his shirt.

He tugged the tails out and seconds later the tailored linen rested on the floor on top of his jacket. She quickly inserted her hands underneath his T-shirt and explored the contours of his chest. His muscles were well defined. His in-and-out breathing had moved to his stomach and pressed against her hands. He flung the white cotton off and it flew through the air.

Oh, my. She had open territory to explore, to touch, and lick. Dare she be so bold? She had wanted to touch his hard cords, so she did. Now, she wanted to taste him. His lips were salty and sweet, pliable and firm. *What would his skin taste like?*

He cupped her breasts, making them full. They came over the split front opening of the dress. Her nipples exploded and pearled in his warm palms. Her heavy sigh morphed into a groan. He tucked his head between her breasts and kissed her skin. Oh, how she wanted him to suck on her nipples. They ached with a need. Maybe if he touched them the wonderful pain would go away.

She leaned her head onto his chest and with a quick swipe of her tongue she licked his tanned skin. The aroma of his cologne, a mix of sandalwood, vanilla, lush floral and sweet amber, switched from a scent into a taste. Beneath the cologne she savored the man. Stein Laxdale tasted like cinnamon.

She lifted her head, intending to take more pleasure, when his fingers stroked her nipple as if her thoughts had been spoken out loud. *Oh!* Instead of easing the ache it throbbed. Liquid pooled where the tingling zinged like a live wire in her vagina. She lifted her legs to wrap around his waist, drawing his penis closer to the place that needed to be filled.

He backed her against the wall, supporting her with his strong thighs. His hands roamed up and down her sides—cupping her breasts, touching the skin. One breast popped out and she hesitated in her explorations of his upper body. What should she do? Before she could think it through he lifted the breast and pressed tiny kisses until he reached the nipple. She could have died right then and there. He rolled his tongue over, under, around, lightly biting and kissed with tiny pecks that made her stomach muscles jump. He massaged the pliable skin around it.

What next? She got her answer when he moved to the other. Scandalous was how she felt with her back pressed against the wall, her bare legs loosely wrapped around his waist, and both of her breasts exposed to his sight and his delectable mouth.

She lowered her hands to his belt, tightened her fingers in the belt loops and pulled his hips closer to her. His penis, firm in his black pants, beckoned her. He stopped suckling her breasts and threw his head back.

Virtuous Kerry McClure remained in Indiana and reckless, bad Kerry occupied her body because for the first time in her life she unfastened a man's belt buckle, unbuttoned and unzipped his trousers until the firm beast behind the brass teeth could be spotted.

She inserted her hand through the opening in his tight black underwear and touched the hard muscle. Her palm rubbed over the top and around the rim. She held the thin bit of skin between her thumb and forefinger, becoming acquainted with the contours. A pearl of fluid came out, thick and slick. He moaned. She glanced into his face. His eyelids were lowered, hiding his beautiful azure eyes. He appeared to be in pain, his lips tight together and his jaw had a tick pulsing.

She lifted her fingers and sniffed the liquid. It smelled a little like sea foam. She touched her index finger to her tongue. The slick, glossy, fluid tasted salty. Not a bad flavor.

"Magda, you're driving me wild. I need you." He grazed his fingers under her dress until she felt him insert them under her silk, thigh-high panties.

Magda.

Her mind, lost in the desire to touch, taste and explore, snapped awake. He called her Magda. She opened her eyes, glanced around the room and moved her arm to stop him from removing her panties. The name badge bit into the tender under skin of her arm.

Magda. He doesn't know who I am. He thinks he's having a one night stand with a fortuneteller. *Stop it. No, gone too far, can't stop. It's what you want too. Do it!*

"Stein, stop. Please." She dropped her legs from around his waist.

He panted and tried to lift her chin with his fingers. She turned away and tucked her breasts back into the evening dress.

"Why?" he whispered, his voice scratchy.

"I'm sorry. I can't explain, but I can't have sex with you." She grabbed her handbag, shawl, and ran out the door.

Chapter Six

Kerry didn't look back. She ran up the five flights of stairs instead of waiting on the elevator. Her body tingled and pulsed in a place previously dormant. She slid the keycard into the lock, walked into the room and quickly shut the door. Leaning against it, she blew out a breath to relax her heart. Jessica's absence was a relief. How could Kerry have explained her disheveled appearance? Wanton! Jezebel!

She had undressed a man. When his hand touched her breasts she leaned into it. Wanted him to touch all of her skin, expose all of it as his gaze had devoured her. She slanted against the wall, dropped her bag onto the foyer table and held her hand to her heart.

A few deep breaths and she stumbled over to the mini-bar. The only beverage was whiskey, not the finest quality and certainly her last choice. She twisted off the cap and threw the amber-colored liquid into the back of her throat. The painful burn made her eyes water, but the fire in her throat hadn't suppressed the need to have Stein's hands touching her.

She grabbed a bottle of water out of the refrigerator and swallowed a fair amount to wash away the liquor. Wash away the memory. A quick pass of her palm over her eyes removed the tears which formed in response to the harshness of the whiskey. Could the tears be a result of her guilt? He probably believed she teased him, took him to the point where he leaked his desire. She lifted her fingers to smell the salty ocean scent again.

The entire scene replayed before her eyes. She visualized the sultry look in his eyes and the hard pulsating muscle under her hand. The taste of him. His scent.

She set the water down, made her way to the bedroom, and grabbed her nightgown. A quick, cold shower would help wash away her longing. In the movies the man always took a long, cold shower to ease his sexual frustration. Maybe it would work for her.

Instead of flipping on the lights above the mirror, she turned on the fan light which provided a soft, hazy glow. A twist of the lever and cold water rained down. She stripped off her dress and undergarments and stepped under the hard spray. Bracing her hands on the tiles, she let the frigid liquid take her breath away.

A quick flick of her fingers and the water went from chilly to warm. She grabbed a washcloth from the stack of fresh linen stacked on the wall rack, soaped it and ran it over her hot-cold skin. A gentle swipe of the rough cloth, so like Stein's fingers, across her breast and her bud peaked. She moved the cotton around the side and underneath.

Realizing what she was doing she shoved her hand against the wall. *Stop it! Why ever are you acting like this? Replicating his actions! Touching yourself as he touched you.* No man had ever created such a stir in her.

She jerked her hand back and cleaned the cloth under the pulsating water. She grabbed the citrus-scented soap and witnessed his image in the soap residue. Two blue specks stood out on the light brown tile, with white soap bubbles capping off his head. In her mind, the likeness of Stein watched her.

She lifted her hand and prepared to wipe the

image away. Her fingers grasped the soap and slid it downward. She wished he could truly be with her at this moment in time. What was he doing?

****

Stein pounded his fist against the wall as he watched her scurry out the door.

"Fuck. Fuck. Fuck."

His cock still upright with glistening bits of cum on the head begged for release. He refastened his trousers, grabbed his T-shirt off the floor and tucked it in as he headed for the door. She'd be at the elevator—if it worked. A turn later and he didn't see her. Where was she? He couldn't decide if she was a tease or inexperienced. She acted as if she'd never seen semen before, and put it in her mouth. Didn't she know the dangers of sexually transmitted diseases? Putting a complete stranger's semen in her mouth wasn't something a practiced woman would do. She had to be an innocent, maybe even a virgin.

A studious, naïve, little librarian had caught his interest and he behaved like a cad. He would find her and make it up to her. He'd fight the feelings of frustration and apologize for his ungentlemanly behavior. Why did he feel this way about her? A firm believer in wooing the woman and getting to know her before pursuing intimacy, he acted out of character. He was a slim-ball. Damn. He'd find her and hope she'd talk to him.

He ran to the set of service elevators. As he passed a woman with a large floppy hat and multicolored dress he twisted so his erection wouldn't be noticed.

The elevator door opened when he approached it. The empty interior reaffirmed he had lost her once again. Asking the people at the front desk would be futile. Jessica. He'd find Jessica and ask her what room Magda stayed in. Did she live in Las Vegas, and if so, where?

He caught the door as it closed, climbed into the lift, and hit the down button. Panic set in when he didn't hear music blasting from the conference room. Thank goodness, revelers continued to mill about. Jukebox songs filtered through the speaker system. Delilah, draped over a Tom Cruise look-a-like, shot him a grin.

He acknowledged her with a nod and continued his search for Magda. Not finding her, he kept to the outer rim of the room and searched for Ian or Jessica. Not spotting either, he cursed the Fates. No, the Fates had given him two encounters; he knew he'd have one more chance. Good things always happened in threes.

He walked into the sultan's tent. A tiny gray-haired woman packed away the crystal ball and tarot cards. "Hi. I'm looking for Magda. Is she here?"

She hiked up the belt so her breasts rested on top of the black band and dragged her eyes down his body and back up again.

"You just missed her. She left about three minutes ago. If you hurry, you can catch her leaving the lobby." She snickered and winked. "If you don't find her, I'll be more than happy to help you with whatever you need." Wink.

"Ah, thank you." Oh god, the woman had to be as old as his grandmother! Well, that certainly killed the last remnants of his erection.

Stein ran out of conference room and into the lobby. Tim wasn't at the desk. A valet stood in front of the entrance.

"Did you see a woman wearing a tight black dress and hauling a brown leather satchel with her?"

"Yes, about fifty women like that in the last ten minutes." He held out a white-gloved hand.

The red-coated valet shoved his open palm out farther. Stein dug into his pants pockets, hoping he had some cash. He withdrew a twenty dollar bill and flattened it into the young man's hand.

The money swiftly disappeared into an inner coat pocket. "She walked, no she hurried, to the right."

Stein rushed past the valet and chugged down the sidewalk, weaving in and out of the late-night visitors. He stopped at the light and glanced right and left. Which way to go? He raced a block down the street, to the other side and back up again. It would be impossible to find her in the thick crowds, especially not knowing which direction she flew. Damn.

He grabbed a brochure from the box on the corner and fanned his hot face. Curling the paper into a tube, he hit it against his thigh as he walked back to the hotel.

As The Hanged Man tarot card indicated, one step back. Tomorrow he would hunt for Magda, make amends and take two steps forward.

In his hotel room, Stein placed the brochure on the counter in the bathroom and turned on the shower. He shed his clothes, flipped on the fan, and the pages from the pamphlet flew open. A quick cool shower would help. Just forget her. *Is she worth the trouble?* The full-color glossy page drew his attention. A dark-eyed naked gypsy lay back on a thick mat of grass. She wore a turban and large gold earrings, and bangles around her wrist and ankles. Between her spread knees was a crystal ball. He slammed the brochure shut and tossed it in the trash can.

His little gypsy was an innocent. He had a week's vacation time to find her, apologize, and date her—if she was willing.

He climbed into the shower and planted Magda's image firmly in his mind, soaped his hand and clutched his dick. Her beautiful face held wonder and enjoyment at touching him, tasting him. He pumped, smoothed, and jerked as he recalled all of her facial expressions. Her naiveté, her curiosity, as she explored his cock. A few tugs later, he found his release.

Tucked under the covers, he replayed the interlude with Magda. Her kisses were hot and responsive. Long fingers with rounded nails stroked him. She seemed innocent in her behavior, but her touch was that of an experienced woman. Yes, she was worth the effort, and tomorrow he would find her.

Chapter Seven

Kerry stirred the packet of dry creamer into her coffee. The air conditioning blew through her cotton tank and shorts, chilling her, despite the early morning sun streaming through the windows. The mountains were beautiful, with pink and purple and gray hues surrounding them, to resemble a Rocket Popsicle, a sweet confection she had had as a child.

"I didn't see a tie on the doorknob last night," Jessica said, joining her at the bar. She wore pink cotton PJ's with a *Hello Kitty* label on the outside. Pink *Hello Kitty* slippers completed the outfit.

"No, couldn't do it. I wanted to, so very much. Don't give me that look, like it's what you expected to happen. It wasn't the same as with Jimmie and I'm not eighteen." She shoved her wet hair behind her ear.

"My engine was revved. He said all the right things, made all the right moves. He fit." Kerry lifted the cup to sip the steaming brew. His kisses made her tingle and his touch created a fire in her, even now, nine hours later.

"He fit?" She poured a cup of coffee.

"We fit. You know, as in just right. Fit." The sweet and earthy pungent scent of the coffee helped with the morning blues. More than their lips fit.

"Uh huh. Fit. So why are you still fidgeting?" Jessica poured a cup of coffee and set it down on the counter table top and waited.

"He thought I was Magda."

"Last night we were all Magda's in that tent.

Cassandra's were in the Cassandra tent. It was a way of keeping the theme and not having people stalk us later."

"I know, but I didn't correct him. Not even after he introduced himself to you, and I knew he had to be *the* Stein Laxdale with Rune Technologies. The same man who saw me without a bra and removed my skirt. I couldn't tell him my true name." She sighed. "It would have been a lie to have had sex with him as Magda."

"Umm hum." Jessica sipped her black coffee.

"What about you and Ian?"

Jessica grimaced. "We didn't fit."

"Want to elaborate?"

"Not right now. How are you going to feel conducting the meeting today? Especially with board member Jeff breathing down your neck."

"Jeff Wanamaker is the least of my worries. I'm hoping you'll be my proxy and lead the meeting." Kerry rushed over to the desk. "Since I didn't get sexual satisfaction last night I made a list of every possible scenario about what could be asked and the response you should make."

"I can't, Kerry," Jessica whispered. "I work with numbers because I'm not a talkative kind of person. I don't deal well with high stress situations involving others. You know people aren't my thing." She crossed her arms at her waist.

Panic set in, Kerry's stomach cramped and her palms began to sweat. She could not bring herself to reveal herself to this man. He kissed her as no other had. He touched her skin and not in the groping fumbling kind of way Jimmie had, no, Stein knew what he was about. She wanted to feel him touch her and to further explore the salty slick muscle beneath his zipper. Could she have that connection men and women have, the one she believed she could have forsaken?

"I'll have to cancel. We'll find another vendor." Kerry turned toward her bedroom. With her hand on the doorknob she stilled.

"There isn't enough time. We've been looking for six months. You've only one week left before your challenge expires," Jessica stammered.

Kerry took her hand from the doorknob and turned to look at her.

"This is so important to you. Do you want to lose to that no good uncle? He'll surely kick you out of the business," Jessica retorted as she dropped her hand from her cup to run her fingers through her blonde locks.

"No, but I can't face Stein. He'll think I knew who he was all along." Kerry bowed her head. The hotel room tableau flashed through her mind. She had undressed him, touched his penis. No she couldn't do it.

"They need this deal. If they get your business, it'll open other possibilities in the United States. They took a risk proposing such outstanding service at an astounding low price. Now you want to jerk it out from under them. So what if the man saw you practically naked. Big deal! There are naked women all over Vegas. You can't let your embarrassment over something so minor ruin your chances, Kerry. *You'll lose everything.*"

"How do you know they need the business?" Kerry's gut clenched in nervous anxiety. She didn't want to lose everything. Yes, she could be happy puttering around her cottage, helping out at the church and living off the income from her McClure Ventures stock, but she wanted to win. She wanted The Garden Center to be as successful as the rest of the enterprises. With a little extra care, she could make the center a place to come for green life again.

Can I do it? Uncertainty popped back into her head, could she walk into that business meeting as a professional and face the man who twisted her stomach into knots? His tongue had delved into her mouth creating a vortex where breathing couldn't occur because her heart pounded so hard in her throat.

"Ian told me about why he was in Las Vegas. He's meeting a man concerning a very important deal for their technology company, to provide servers and storage."

"A man?" Kerry wiped her palms against the cotton of her top.

"This isn't the first time someone's mistaken your identity based on the spelling of your name. People assume Kerry is a man's name unless it's spelled with an i."

"That's it. I'll be a man, and he won't know me as Magda. This city is known for costumes. Do you think I could get someone — yes, one of Mom's old friends, to dress me as a man? Ramon could work his magic and create make-up and enhancements."

Jessica's face lit as bright as the sun now warming Kerry's cold skin. Jessica apparently did fit with Ian, if she wanted them to be successful. Or else, leading a business meeting did indeed terrify her.

"Yes. Call. Call now." Jessica grabbed the cell from the charger on the foyer table and handed it to Kerry.

Chapter Eight

"Is the voice box covered by the ascot?" Kerry asked.

"For the third time, yes. You sound like Froggie from the old black and whites we watched at two in the morning." Jessica reached over and straightened the lapels of Kerry's blue and brown tweed suit.

"Ready."

"Let's go, we've kept them waiting for twenty minutes already." Jessica adjusted the computer bag on her shoulder. Kerry threw open the door.

"Who the hell are you?" A high-pitched, male voice screeched as he rose from the chair.

"Damn, forgot to warn board member Jeff," Jessica whispered from behind.

"Jeff, would you step into the hallway for a moment please," Kerry said in her replicated smoker's voice. She stepped back and let Jessica stand in the doorway.

He glanced at Jessica and then, thankfully, he hauled his thin, white body around her friend and out into the hallway. Jessica stepped in and the door shut, leaving Kerry to fend for herself.

"Jeff, it's me, Kerry. The men inside think I'm a man. I want the deal to go down, and if it means I have to pretend to be a guy then I will."

"You're lying to them?" He shoved a hairless hand through his thinning hair. He resembled an otter in his brown suit and squinty eyes.

"No, I'm just giving them the image they expect. It won't change the contracts in any way." *Nor am I doing anything morally wrong*, she told herself. Although her stomach clenched, she hadn't quite converted into believing the ruse was ethical—even if it would end in a win-win situation.

Stein watched the woman nervously shuffle papers around in her bag and jerk a laptop from its case.

"Hi, Jessica, how are you this afternoon?"

"I'm fine and thank you for asking, Stein. Since you don't seem surprised to see me here, I assume you've connected my name with McClure Ventures."

She hadn't met his gaze and failed to acknowledge Ian. Something didn't smell right with this entire setup.

Why did the board member not recognize Kerry McClure, the CEO? Shit, he needed the deal, but wouldn't get involved in anything dishonest. He wanted a good reputation in America, not some scam related benchmark. When he'd done the research on the company, although they had an impressive portfolio, he couldn't find photos of Kerry McClure. Seeing the tiny, emaciated man in person with sleek black hair and pasty white skin, he understood why.

"Actually, Ian made the connection," Stein said.

Jessica finally looked up, and her blue eyes held a hint of sadness. "Good morning, Ian. How are you today?"

What happened last night between those two? Stein planned to find out, especially if it affected their business deal.

"Fine, just fine." Ian jumped from his seat and went to the credenza. A glass rattled and clinked as the water carafe connected with it.

"Didn't get your five-mile run in, old man?" Stein asked quietly, as he joined him.

"No, I decided a run wasn't what I needed." Ian glanced toward the table. The sound of a PC booting up chimed in the air. "Frustrated is what I'd call myself." A frown creased his face.

"Ah," Stein whispered. "It's about damn time."

"I don't know what you're talking about, bloke." Water sloshed over the glass as Ian walked back to the table.

"Aiteas," Stein murmured in Gaelic. Strange, the entire Vegas experience has been strange.

The short man, Kerry McClure, came through the door followed by Jeff Wanamaker. Stein sat beside Ian. "Do you believe he's the prominent board member of McClure Ventures? Wanamaker asserts he makes the decisions for the company."

"That's what he claims. I guess we'll find out once we talk with *The McClure*," Ian said, keeping his voice hushed.

Stein knew better because he had weekly email sessions with Kerry McClure. Kerry, a force to be reckoned with, would make the decisions and not some simpering board member.

"Hello, gentlemen, I'm Kerry McClure," he extended a tiny but hairy hand. He noticed because it was gorilla hairy. Stein glanced at Ian, who wore an expression of distaste. McClure's shoulders moved from side to side as if stiffness affected his mobility. Not wanting to offend him, Stein gave a quick shake. A little bit of pressure and it was over. Ian resumed his seat and gave a head nod.

"I want to personally thank you both for coming today, especially for traveling from Dublin to Las Vegas. Yearly, I attend a benefit in honor of my mother, and it coincided with our meeting. I hope you'll enjoy your stay at *Yellow Fever*. Your rooms have been paid for by McClure Ventures. Were you able to include some vacation time in as well?"

McClure bumped his belly into the side of the table and Ian's water glass splashed liquid onto the flat silver surface.

"Yes, Mr. McClure, we have arranged a few days

for a holiday. We've enjoyed the scenery so far." Stein smiled and backed up his chair. The odd little man smelled like starched cotton and cheap cologne. The scent, anything but pleasant, wafted across the table.

"Please, call me Kerry. You've met a member of our board, Jeff Wanamaker, and this is our accountant, Jessica Hoke. Jessica, have you introduced yourself?"

She nodded.

"Yes, well let's get down to the basics. From our last conversation I've a few questions, which need to be answered." McClure shuffled papers in front of him and picked up an ink pen.

Stein anticipated a different version of McClure. From his emails he'd sounded young, energetic, and personable. This enigma wore a thick wool coat, the cotton of his shirt was so tightly bound it was impossible to see how he could breathe under all that weight. His black hair shone like glossy plastic.

Despite his small stature, he had a forceful way about him and his voice brooked no argument. At least that preconceived idea of what Stein expected proved to be true.

The management questions were easy to answer. As the tech person, Ian responded to the queries about installation and maintenance. He also reviewed the communication process connecting all of the ventures to a primary server and the benefits of the email server they would provide. McClure's glance met Stein's. Kerry squirmed in his seat, shifting from side to side. Occasionally, Jeff would slip a condescending smirk toward Kerry. McClure ignored him. Something wasn't right, Stein once again questioned if it could be a setup.

"That concludes all the questions I have. Jessica, do you or Jeff have any thing to add?" Kerry's voice rattled and a slight buzzing came from his neck.

What the hell? Stein definitely had reservations after viewing the old codger's face. He stood and leaned over the table. "It seems you've a bit of smoke coming from your neck."

Stein grabbed Ian's glass. "Here's some water if you need it. Damn, are you on fire?"

He set the glass down and started to move around the table. The strange man, despite his advanced age, quickly rose and with a slight nod of his head glanced at Jessica. The sleeves of his jacket fell over his wrist. An odd, rancid scent infiltrated the air. He lifted his hand to his neck and shuffled toward the door.

Jessica coughed and stuffed her PC into the padded bag. "I don't have any questions. Jeff?"

Those had to be the most words the woman had spoken during the entire meeting, enough to fill a Post-it Note. She closed her bag, appearing as if she prepared to run out of the room.

"As if it mattered," Jeff muttered.

"Now is the time to ask questions, Mr. Wanamaker," Stein said.

Wanamaker glanced at McClure's retreating back. He narrowed his eyes and pushed his chair from the table. It bumped and squeaked as it ground against the gold marble floor.

"If you'd provide me with a copy of the final evaluation, I'll look it over." He stood and shoved the chair up to the table.

Strange.

McClure stopped at the door and turned to look at them. "Well, then, we accept Rune Technology's proposal. If you write up an agreement and fax it to me by the end of the day tomorrow, we have a deal."

"Jessica will give you the details about the fax, etcetera." McClure nodded. Jessica gathered McClure's papers with scribbled notes on it, as the tiny fellow shuffled out of the room. No, Stein amended, McClure ran from the room.

"Nice to meet you and Jeff," Stein said, he lifted his hand to shake their hands. The lingering brimstone scent from McClure's wake flowed up his nostrils.

Mr. Wanamaker frowned as he quickly followed McClure.

"Kerry had to catch a plane back to Lantern, Indiana." Jessica withdrew a business card and gave it to him. She smiled a small, bashful parting of the lips, and slipped out of the room. The rapid click of her heels echoed as she flew down the hallway.

"Aiteas," Ian said.

"Very strange, but alainn," Stein replied. And she was beautiful, but not as breathtaking as Magda.

"She's mine," Ian said.

"I couldn't tell it," Stein laconically replied.

"She twists my insides. Are you happy? Yes, I want her. For the first time in my life I want to be with a woman instead of having a good time. You were trying to dig it out of me earlier, right?" He ran shaking fingers through his hair. "I thought she'd be an easy, ah, date, but she clammed up at the mention of a romp in my room."

"Playing hard to get?"

"No, she's certainly not playing hard to get. I'm not sure what her deal is—yet." Ian gathered his notes and stuffed them into his portfolio. "Good thing you wrote up the agreement anticipating success."

Stein smiled. "Yes. Although McClure isn't what I expected, he did his research and knew what questions to ask."

"Yes, some of the tech questions took me my surprise." Ian gathered the papers and meandered toward the exit. "But I can't get past the grossness of the blighter."

McClure's oddity didn't muck the rewards, they had the contract. "You handled it. Now, we can get rid of Maeve, and enjoy the rest of our holiday," Stein replied.

****

"What do you mean they were all Magdas?" Stein yelled into the hotel phone.

"I'm sorry, Mr. Laxdale, but the event was designed as a fantasy. The theme made it a success. Because we chose a *fantasy*, we made all the volunteers Magdas, Cassandras, and Delilahs to protect them from unwanted overtures. If your Magda wanted you to know her *real* name, she would have shared it with you." The snippy librarian's voice rattled through the phone wire. "Good day, Mr. Laxdale."

"Did you hear?" Stein replaced the receiver on the set.

"Who couldn't hear? I think the maid next door in my room heard." Ian slid his hands into the pockets of his shorts and stared out the window. "She's gone."

"Who?" Stein asked.

"Jessica," Ian said, his voice so sad it made the bright celebratory day seem overcast. "She and McClure hopped a plane back to Indiana immediately after the meeting."

"Is it important for you to see Jessica again?" Stein asked. It wasn't like Ian to be so into a lass. He had a reputation as a ladies man, not a one-woman man.

"The best sex I've ever had."

"I thought you said she didn't want to have a go at it," Stein retorted.

"She scoffed at going to my room, but the service elevator seemed to turn her on."

Stein raised an eyebrow.

"Cut it out." Ian walked over to the window in

the room. "We'd been to dinner, then dancing, and on our way up to our rooms. The main elevator had a crowd in front of it, so I took a page from your book, and we went to the service elevator. It didn't get stuck much to my disappointment." He pivoted and crossed his arms. "Until it bumped to a stop, and she fell onto me. I wrapped my arms around her promising her, ah, safety. No one entered, the doors closed and we..."

Ian withdrew a soda from the fridge. He flipped the tab and took a swallow.

"And? It broke down?" Stein's own elevator experience flashed through his mind. The memory of the soft pressure of Magda's lips and her smooth firm legs on his shoulders sent a rush through his body. She was brave and had a fabulous sense of humor. Desire ramped through his body.

"Well, I'm not one to kiss and tell, but too bad you couldn't have gotten it on with the fortuneteller because elevator sex is hot and the climax builds fast."

"Damn, you're so lucky. And now you want to see her again?" Stein twirled the room's keycard between his fingers.

"Yes," Ian whispered.

"She didn't act very friendly toward you today." Stein tightened his lips.

"I think she had a connection with me. I'd like to see her again outside the glitz and glamour of Las Vegas to determine if the shimmer and freshness of what had begun last night could last."

Stein was thinking similar thoughts of seeing Magda outside of her gypsy tent and the hotel. He wanted to take her on a normal date.

"I must say, seeing you so excited over the prospect of a committed relationship is far more interesting than Las Vegas and something I wouldn't want to miss. I'm up for a bit of adventure with the fairer sex. I say good-bye Las Vegas, hello, Lantern, Indiana." Stein dragged his luggage from the closet and placed it on the bed. "I'll hand deliver the agreement to McClure Ventures. You'll get to see Jessica. Maybe I'll be able to convince the woman to tell me the name of her elusive librarian friend. Call the airlines. We can be there tonight or tomorrow morning at the latest."

Chapter Nine

The next day, Kerry stared at her summer intern as he stood with his back to the flatbed full of shrubs and perennials. McClure Ventures took on at least two interns each summer. They generally worked with the corporate office concerning sales and marketing the paper products line, but Bobby wanted to experience the ins and outs of conservation.

Public sales at The Garden Center proved to be an excellent starting point for him. He would get information, finding out what the general public requested in the line of plant life and their conservation habits if he asked the right questions. Perhaps the customer would be educated as well.

"...let Skinny do it. Okay, Kerry?" he repeated with a slight edge to his voice.

Irritable and holding unkind thoughts, she withheld the smart retort to his benign question. Her lack of patience, a direct result of her time in Vegas, made her listening skills inadequate. The contract deal with Stein didn't sit well with her. Even lighting a candle and asking forgiveness for lying didn't relieve her guilt. In addition, she couldn't get their encounter in the hotel room out of her system. She still wanted him. She should have completed the act when she had the opportunity.

"Miss Kerry, I'm going into the store to get a drink of water," Bobby said. The clever man changed tactics, as a liter of water was within a few feet.

Kerry and her intern had only been moving

shrubs for a mere ten minutes. How hard could it be for him to move the plants off the wagon bed and onto a display rack? Damn, immature twenty-year-old. *Oh my, I sound like my father.*

A youngster. She chuckled. He was only five years younger. Why did she suddenly feel so much older? Lost in her thoughts she didn't hear him the second time.

"Miss Kerry, I need to take a break." Bobby stood, his elbows jutting out from his waist and one jean clad leg cocked to the side. Sweat dripped along the sides of his handsome face and onto the collar of his cotton, button-down shirt.

It would be interesting to see how dedicated to the business he considered himself. Being book smart helped to understand the process, but most great leaders began at the bottom and worked their way up. She'd help him learn the details of a product, and in this case The Garden Center.

He'd get to know the different aspects of the Center, from seed to plant and into the customer's hand, before he went to the conservation center to learn about marketing the not-for-profit. He shouldn't be shot down because of her mistakes.

"Sure, take ten minutes. After we're done with the shrubs we need to set up a garden pond over by the arbor." Kerry nodded to him. She stifled the urge to smile as he groaned.

Relax. She'd rushed the kid, exhausted him. Maybe her motivation to hard labor resulted from sexual frustration and disappointment about not revealing her true self to Stein. She picked up the arborvitae shrub and set it on the wooden platform. The bush shook, hitting the branches of the greenery beside it. Cedar infiltrated the air. She hadn't worked this hard since her father passed away eleven months ago. The rhythm of moving the plants, the scent of the pine and fresh-turned soil relaxed her.

She wiped the sweat off her forehead. Tomorrow her muscles would ache, but as a manager she believed in leading by example, so she'd be sore and not complain. Until they got the stock unloaded and the displays arranged she, and maybe her intern, would continue to toil.

The hard work relieved the anxiety she'd gained over the past few days. She smiled at the memory as she told her uncle he might have lost. Maybe this time next week she'd be officially appointed CEO of McClure Ventures.

Another shrub, heavier than the last, landed with a loud thud on the platform. She was hearing Stein's voice in the wind now. Heaven sent, it was.

Obtaining the Rune Technology service, beneficial to McClure Ventures, would make her CEO appointment firm. Kerry may have been able to get the board to appoint her without the technology deal, but it made for a sure indictment. Could she wait five days to find out if she got the appointment? Kerry bent over to grab another plant and got lost in the pace of moving the shrubs from the wagon to the platform.

"Excuse me, miss," his accented lyrical voice shouted.

So focused on her next move concerning her Uncle Mike, she hadn't heard Stein's voice until he shouted near her ear. Kerry stiffened as she smelled the scent of his familiar cologne. The sandalwood mixed with his unique male scent made her stomach muscles jump and jerk.

The lilt in his lovely Irish voice made her sexual awakening manifest. Moisture tingled between her legs and glancing at her breasts she found them swelled and pointed. The yearning to connect with him hadn't been burnt off with the sweat from exercise. She couldn't face him. Would he hate her for deceiving him? If she turned around and saw him, she'd be lost. Yet, the desire to reveal her true self was paramount. What to do?

Stooped in a bent over position, she hoped he'd walk away. He didn't.

"Excuse me," he said louder, slower, plainer. "I'm looking for Mr. McClure. The clerk inside said Kerry would be in the perennial area. Have you seen him?"

Kerry remained bent over the plant and shook her head. *Chicken.*

"Kerry," Bobby shouted.

The scruffy little woman refused to acknowledge him. Stein had met several Midwesterners and thought they were a friendly lot. Apparently not! From the back she looked like a teenager, with her shiny dark brown pony tail trailing out from the hole in her baseball cap. Her shirt indicated she was an advocate of a five kilometer foot race event. It had several supporters written in white on the dark blue background. Why wouldn't she turn around? He slipped the envelope holding the agreement into his pocket and reached out.

His hand wrapped around her bare, tightly muscled arm, and made her turn to face him. When he touched her she tensed, as if he had frightened her. A smudge of dirt crossed from her nose to her right ear. She wore no makeup, her face sweaty and as innocent as Madonna. A small round burn mark about the size of a quarter was on the center of her neck. She lowered her eyelids and licked her lips.

Damn, he recognized her—the gypsy.

"Magda," he whispered as he took a step forward intending to wrap her into his arms.

"Kerry," the guy loudly stated.

Her eyelids shot open. Stein glanced at her face, at her neck, and her height. He shifted his focus to the young man addressing her, and then back to her dewy eyes. He dropped his hand.

"Kerry McClure?" he hissed. His heart pounded as fast as the electric hoot owl screeching next to them. She'd lied to him. Deceived him. Used him.

"Stein, I can explain."

"I'm sure you can. I'm surprised you didn't go ahead and sleep with me to get what you wanted. I know you craved sex. Was it a game to you? Masked seduction? I'd have been willing to agree to your demands but now, the deal's off."

He turned to leave. No, not good enough. The anger grew and with a sudden move, he whirled around and clasped her arms.

"No, as a matter of fact." He pulled her into a hug. "I've changed my mind. I'll have sex with you. You'll get a good deal and a guarantee as well."

She kept her gaze focused on him. Moisture formed and glazed over her pretty brown eyes. *Damn.* He released her.

"I can see by your expression you don't want to finish what you started in Vegas. Just as well. Good-bye, Kerry McClure." He walked away, leaving her to deal with the tears, the remorse, and the regret. If she had it in her.

"It wasn't like that. Let me explain. Please." Her teary voice joined the owl's screech. A small hand clamped onto his wrist and tugged him away from the gawking young man.

Kerry stood with her legs braced apart. She tilted the blue cap with white letters spelling out McClure Ventures on the bill and crossed her arms over her waist.

"It's all a big misunderstanding. I didn't know who you were when we were trapped in the elevator. I was working as Magda in the tent. We all wore name badges that said Magda as part of the theme and for protection. We didn't want others to know our real names. The situation escalated out of control." Her lips quivered, and she clamped her tiny white teeth on the lower one.

"Drunks like the one who entered the tent, I understand. I don't know why you didn't tell me your real name, especially after you knew mine." He imitated her stance and straightened his back. His height overpowered her. Stein was angry enough he wanted to intimidate her, reject her. He refused to play the fool.

She narrowed her eyes. "You saw me in the elevator without a bra, took off my skirt. I couldn't transact business with someone who had seen me so unprofessionally."

"That explains some. What about dancing? And later? You could have told me after we, ah, kissed. It wasn't business then, or was it?" he snarled, feeling the ache deep within because he thought their connection, attraction, had been real.

"I wanted to be with you," she whispered and dropped her hands to her sides.

"Ms. McClure, I need help with a customer. She only wants to talk to you," the young man said, two feet away from them. He held a pair of gloves in his hand and pounded them against his leg. Why were his lips pulled together in a tight line? Jealousy? Were they lovers?

"Stein, we need to talk," she pleaded. Her eyes held sincerity. She lifted her hand toward him.

"I'll leave you, Ms. McClure. I'm sure you'll make it with another firm." He hoped his sarcastic remark would take root.

"Fine then, have it your way, you stubborn ass." She tugged the cap firmly on her head and shot past him. The breeze blew her citrus scent into his nostrils, reawakening his desire and the memory of his mouth suckling her soft, scented breasts.

****

"That's the story. I left when the kid

approached. She's a liar, a sneak, and a tease." Stein paced in the hotel room.

"What will you tell Maeve?" Ian asked from his vigil at the window.

"We'll go to our second option, liquidate the business and start a new company under a different name. Maeve will get her cut of the business, and she'll be out of our lives."

Ian pivoted around. Hands tucked in his pockets, he glared at Stein. "Reconsider. We'll need another deal before the end of the month in order to buy her out. If we start from scratch it'll take us at least three years to balance and another two before we make profits."

"I don't see that we have a choice." Stein removed the letter of agreement out of his pocket and placed it on the entry table.

"McClure Ventures is a reputable company. I'm confident the corporation will fulfill their end of the deal. I think you should submit the contract directly to Jeff Wanamaker."

Stein took a swig of the soda he'd found in the hotel fridge, and contemplated the words. Ian was correct. He shouldn't let a woman affect his business, his financial responsibilities. He had before and look where it'd gotten him.

"Fine. I'll let you take the contract to them."

"Great. I'll take it right now. What about Kerry?" Ian asked.

Stein met his stare. Ian lifted a brow.

"Kerry means nothing to me." Stein's gut clenched in protest as the words went flying from his mouth. She did. He continued to want her and imagined them coming to terms. But right now, he let his anger rule his head. Logically, he shouldn't love her.

What man meets a woman and knows, beyond a shadow of a doubt, they belonged together? What man falls in love with a sexy little gypsy after spending twenty minutes alone with her in a dark elevator?

None! At least he'd never met one.

Yet the pain around his heart burned.

"So you're willing to sacrifice the woman?" Ian asked, walking over to the mirror to straighten his tie.

"She lied to me, misled me." Stein plopped onto the paisley green and gold chair by the window.

"Come on, we'll take the contract over and then go on a piss," Ian said, with an encouraging smile. "I'm sure they have an excellent dark beer in the hotel bar downstairs."

"I thought you had arranged a date with Jessica?"

"I'll postpone until tomorrow. You need to get drunk—drown the sorrows and all that." Ian opened his cell phone.

Three soft taps sounded on the door. Stein prayed it wasn't Kerry for round two, and hoped it was Kerry. Thoughts of the bed nearby filled his head with all the delectable things he'd love to do to her.

"I'll get it." Stein jumped up from the chair.

Stein opened the door to find Jessica on the other side.

"Good evening, Mr. Laxdale."

"Why so formal? Oh, yes, you talked to Magda —or rather Kerry." Stein moved to the side, gave a slight bow and held his arm out as an invitation for her to enter. She glided into the room. He closed the door as Ian slid his cell phone into the belt clip. The intensity of Jessica and Ian's gazes made Stein crave a toss in the sack with a woman of his own—no— only Kerry could fill that void.

"I don't want to keep you two from your date. Have a good time," Stein spat. His voice came out sharp and brittle, even to his own ears. Anger ruled, because of his foolishness, anger at Kerry, and anger at himself for continuing to picture her in his mind and in his arms.

Jessica whirled on him so fast her flawlessly groomed hair stood straight out from her head. The scent of her floral perfume spread out in the space around her as she pointed a perfectly manicured red fingernail at Stein.

"I've had enough with the both of you. You and Kerry are obviously attracted to each other. It's a simple case of misunderstanding. She was embarrassed. You thought she was a male. Rune Technologies needed the deal, and Kerry wanted the security in order to be appointed CEO. Both of you could get what you want out of the business agreement." Her face was tight with rage as she smoothed the skirt of her dress.

"Now, go find a relationship out of the rubble of your misunderstandings." Her red high-heel tapped a quick cadence on the carpeted floor. The scent of cinnamon from her breath coursed over him when she came within inches of his face. "Don't be a jerk, call her. She's crying over you."

Stein's jaw hardened. He bit back the retort concerning the misunderstanding statement. There wasn't confusion; Kerry knew exactly what she was doing. Ian frowned at him. Jessica handed Stein a white envelope and within two steps threw open the door and stormed into the passageway.

"Don't be acting the arse," Ian said as he grabbed the door. "Call her. Better yet, get a box of bleeding candy and a rack of flowers and take them to her."

The door shut and Stein plopped down on the bed. He propped the thick, stuffed pillows behind his head and crossed his feet with enough force to make the bed bounce.

"Women are nothing but trouble."

He slit the envelope and withdrew the card, a tarot card.

The Hanged Man glared at him through narrowed eyes. He flipped the card over and read what was written on the back in flowing calligraphy: End a struggle, give up control, change your mind even if it means sacrifice, and take one step back and two steps forward. Underneath, in precise small feminine handwriting was Kerry's home phone number and address.

She lived on Mystical Lane. He'd find out what her story was.

Chapter Ten

"Kerry, are you sure you're going to be all right alone? I can stay if you need me," Bobby said. His voice sounded loud in her head. She glanced over at him, a mere two inches away.

Like a water-color painting, the details of his face smeared before her eyes. Thankfully, his hands, steady on her waist, held her upright.

"No, I'll be fine. Thank you for taking me to the hospital. The doctor said it was just a little muscle pull. The shoulder should be back to normal in a day or two. Rest." She tapped his face with her finger, like a mother who's trying to make a point with her child. "I appreciate your concern. Take tomorrow off. You worked hard today."

His eyes held a hint of humor amid the concern. "You're smiling like you've been on a bender. I hate to leave you alone."

"No worries, I'll make it on my own. Have for years. Can for another twenty if needed," she airily replied. "I made a silly mistake—lifted without using my thighs—stupid. Let anger rule."

The cool, numbing ointments, the anti-inflammatory pain pill, and the muscle relaxant drug would wear off, but for now she didn't have a care in the world. The nursing staff had to cut off one side of her T-shirt was open to her waist. Her head had to weigh at least twelve pounds as it fell to her warm, bare right shoulder. As it hit the surface abrasion, fresh pain surged and she jerked.

"Jesus, Kerry, I wish you weren't my boss," he

hissed. His hand tightened on her waist as he led her to the sleek brown sofa. The suede material appeared as soft as mink in her fog, and she couldn't wait to lay on it.

"I'll try to be a better one. I've had a rough day. Please don't be nice to a lonely old maid. I don't deserve it." *Pathetic.* Could she get any more pathetic? *Let the kid go and stop feeling sorry for yourself.* She sat on the sofa, and he took a step back.

"I didn't mean that, I meant you're, ah... never mind." He shoved his hand through his hair. "Do you need anything before I leave? The ice pack has melted, and it's about time for heat."

"Nope. Feeling good. I'll be fine. Shower and bed." Her head fell against the couch. She felt grimy and a couple of her fingernails were broken to the quick from lifting the heavy cement planter. At least the planter hadn't shattered when it fell. The Center would need all the income it could get if she didn't get the CEO position. Her Uncle Mike would surely sell it straightaway because the Center wasn't making a profit yet.

Of all of the companies in the venture, she loved The Garden Center the most. She needed it to survive because it kept her close to her roots. The paper industry, conservation venues, and other endeavors great and small were all profitable. The Garden Center was the only venture in jeopardy. She wouldn't let it fail. She'd take her funds and invest in it and dedicate her services, full time. Maybe she could find another technology company to help her before the date of expiration. Perhaps the board would appoint her as CEO without the deal.

"I'll check on you tomorrow before I go to the Garden Center," he said, his voice sounding very far away. She'd forgotten he was in the room.

She lifted her head and attempted to gaze into

his hazel eyes. "Thanks. Don't need to worry about me. I'm sure I'll be dandy in the morning."

"The doctor told you to rest your shoulder for at least two days." He sat down beside her and he eased her upright. A spasm rushed through her arm, but she didn't care.

"What do they know? I might take tomorrow off. I'll see how I feel in the morning." The Nirvana-like numbness tingling through her gave her a sense of *don't care about nothing*. She could lift an entire house.

Kerry tapped him on the cheek. "You're a cutie. Thanks for helping me today. Oh, you're a pretty color of red."

If possible his face grew even redder.

"Sorry, unprofessional. I seem to be saying all the wrong things today." She sighed and let her head drop back to the sofa. Paper crinkled and plastic bottles knocked together as he stood.

"I'll put the drugs they gave you on the counter in the kitchen near the sink. Do you have over the counter pain relievers in case you need something before your next dose of the stuff the doctor gave to you?"

"Yep. Got it covered, they're already out on the countertop because of a headache earlier. Thanks again. Leave now, so I can get some rest. But first, a shower."

The bottles of pills rattled as he carried them down the hallway. Maybe it was the drugs that caused her to be so loopy. She glanced around through a kaleidoscope haze.

Her compact cottage had excellent use of space. The massive windows allowed the last light of day in, to warm the interior. She stretched, soaking up the evening rays before the sun completely disappeared. What a beautiful night. Yet, her heart continued to ache. She missed him. If only...

"I'll call you tomorrow to see if you need anything. Jessica said she'd try to stop by later."

"Yep, Jessica's my friend. She loves Ian. Ian loves her." Sadness welled within her.

"Yes, well, we'll talk about that another day. If you don't need anything else..." Bobby's voice sounded farther away.

"Nope, all's good." Kerry sighed.

"Bye."

"Good night. Godspeed," she said.

The door shut, once again leaving her alone. She eased off the sofa and sniffed. Definitely a shower next. The mixture of dirt, perspiration, and medicinal scents, repulsed her sensitive nose. The sharp pains from the pulled muscle pierced down her arm.

She walked into the kitchen and picked up one of the four bottles. *Need a pain killer.* Umm, which one was for pain and which one was for relaxation? Tucking one of the brown plastic pill containers into the sling and grabbing an opened bottle of water, she held the bottle between her good arm and her chest. She pressed and twisted the cap to open the vial with oxy written on it. What a cute word oxy. *Oxy moxy. Oxymoron. Oxybillboxy.* Chuckles left her throat as she tried to get the darn thing open. She went into the bedroom and sat on the edge of the bed.

Why would the good pill gurus make it so difficult to get into the bottle? She placed the water on the bedside table and held the container between her knees. A twist and groan later they went flying over the wooden surface. Darn. She took the other bottle out of her sling and placed it among the pills. She threw two tablets into her mouth, took a drink of water and headed for the bathroom.

In her bathroom she unfastened the Velcro sling, dropped it and her clothes onto the floor. She turned the shower head to pulsating. No gentle rain tonight.

The water rose to the torrid temperature she desired. Doctor's orders heat-cold, cold-heat. A quick brush of her teeth got rid of that fuzzy mouth feeling. She touched the burn at her neck, an embarrassment. The ER doctor hadn't bought the story that a piece of hot metal flew up and hit her. She wanted to say, *the voice modulation device malfunctioned when I was trying to pass myself off as a man.* No doubt the good doctor noted a concern for her burned neck in her chart.

Given time she'd somehow get her integrity back. Small white lies every once in a while were okay if it was to protect someone, but she'd been telling outright whoppers for the past three days. She'd take the time to find her candor, to intelligently consider the facts and have the courage to talk to people directly. Maybe she should ask others for their opinions before making decisions. She had become sinfully arrogant.

The mirror reflected a wide-eyed girl whose face appeared as white as bleached linens. She wanted to laugh at how her pupils looked like tiny pin-points. *Idiot, tugging at that cement planter didn't help to get rid of the misery, did it? But he had hurt her.* What had she expected? She lied to him. He'd been honest with her. From the emails she'd built up a trust, and then in one stupid move she'd crushed her carefully constructed opportunity.

Kerry climbed into the marble tiled shower. She placed both hands on the sides for support, and then jerked the injured shoulder back into place. She soaked her aching muscles. Limited to one hand, she scrubbed her hair with the fresh jasmine-scented shampoo and conditioner. A few squirts of verbena scented liquid down her body, she did the best she could. Hopefully the verbena, a stress reliever, would kick in and help her relax.

Stein's reaction, insulting, created fury in her. She touched her lips where he kissed her in anger, but with a gentle force, almost like he wanted to be annoyed but lacked the willpower.

Her arm had a little more flexibility as she shut off the water. She walked out of the shower and snuggled into a towel. After a few quick swipes of the wide-tooth comb through her hair, one-handed she pumped body lotion from the container. It sprayed over the sink and onto the mirror. Enough collected on her fingers to smear the lotion on her dry face. If she could get past the image of Stein's vehemence and disappointment, maybe sleep would occur.

Were her ears ringing? Had the hospital overmedicated her? When she ran competitive events and had muscle pulls, she had never felt this woozy from taking a muscle-relaxant. She shook her head, when the sound came again. The doorbell.

Couldn't be Jessica, must be Bobby. She shuffled toward the entrance using the wall as support. As a minimalist, she didn't have to worry about knocking a lot of art work off the wall. The bell rang again, dong, dong, dong vibrated through her head. *Cripes, I need to get a new chime.*

The door, heavy oak, was difficult to tug open. "Bobby, I'll be fine."

She swayed, totally off balance from the heat of the shower, the ringing in her head, and the stress of opening the door. Or maybe, because of who stood in front of her.

Chapter Eleven

"Are you steamed?" Stein barked.

"Nope, happy as can be." She sucked up the tears threatening to break out. The crying jag had ended five hours ago, so why did they now rest again at the hub of her tear ducts?

She thought she was over it.

Over him.

Guess not.

"Goodbye, Stein." Kerry pushed the door.

He stopped the solid oak with his large hand. "Are you plastered? You can hardly stand straight, and you answered the blasted door wearing only a towel."

"None of your business. Why are you here? You said you never wanted to see me again." Kerry had to sit down. The pills, the exhaustion, and the stress overwhelmed her, in addition to seeing two of him. Two identical Steins would kill her.

"What is wrong with you?" he bellowed as he slipped through the door. His glance shifted from the main room down the hallway. "Are you alone?"

His loud voice created a rising gurgle in her stomach. She would hurl. She turned and weaved with an unsteady gait to the sofa. Lying on her side, she pulled her knees up to her stomach. The couch did feel like mink.

"Good night, Stein, take your two heads and close the door on your way out." Her voice sounded husky and other than the reverberation in her ears, silence pervaded.

"Please," she whispered. The tears hovering at the corners of her eyes slipped over and ran down her face, pooling on the beige lap blanket askew on the sofa. She closed her eyes, trying to stop her snuffles, when she heard the door click shut.

His cool smooth fingers touched her face. She pulled her bottom lip between her teeth to prevent the sob lodged in her throat from erupting.

"Love, what happened?" His soothing, lyrical voice spread warmth through her.

She opened her eyes. If she could remove the knot of the towel without loosing it, she'd wipe her face and rant about his unprofessional behavior. But his fingers were soft, and his eyes showed apprehension.

He cared for her, and she him.

She couldn't deny the connection.

"I pulled a shoulder muscle. Bobby, my student intern, drove me to the hospital. I took a muscle relaxant which has rendered me powerless. Now, please leave. I'm not up for battling with you tonight. I'll be fine."

"Aye, right." He wiped away a tear as it slid down her face.

"Please don't be nice to me. I'm not done being angry at you."

"I've been thick as a brick, and I want to talk to you. But, I see you're shagged-out, so I'm going to carry you to bed." He picked her up as if she were a delicate bundle of flowers, one arm supporting her lower back and the other under her knees, leaving her shoulder pain free.

His course didn't veer, direct and steady he carried her to her bedroom. *How did he know? Ah, yes, the only room with a light on.* She snuggled close to his chest, feeling secure for the first time in days.

He stopped inside the bedroom. "I like your decorating style."

"I like simple," she said, glancing around at the relaxing sage green walls and multicolored accents, which created the illusion of the outdoors, inside.

"I'm a simple man, Kerry." He shifted her weight in his arms.

"Generally, I'm an honest person," she whispered.

Her wet hair swung to the side, as he lowered her legs to the floor.

"I know, love." Stein swallowed. Mesmerized by watching his throat moved up and down, she catapulted further into the lust zone.

"The towel's wet, you'll need to lose it." He kept her anchored by one hand and jerked the coverlet down with the other.

"Oh, clothes. I can't believe this is the second time I've been nearly naked with you and have yet to have sex."

"When were you almost naked?" His brows jumped in a comical, yet seductive manner.

"Hotel."

"Right. If you sit on the bed you won't topple onto the floor will you?"

"Nope, completely fine. Nothing can bother me. All good." She sat down. "I'm getting hot though." She lifted her hands to the towel, she tugged at the knot.

"Kerry, please." He cleared his throat. "Please do not remove the towel until I have something for you to put on."

She raised her glance and sought an answer in his pain-filled eyes. Her gaze trailed down to his pants to find his penis fully erect. Could she convince him to make love to her, not as a business deal but as a woman needing to be loved?

"Stein?" One hand touched the knot, as the other reached out to him.

He jumped back, and her arm dropped like an

anvil to her side. She lowered her head. The towel held steady by her full, aching breasts.

"I know, love." He took two steps forward and lifted her chin with two fingers. "There's nothing I want more than to make long, slow love to you right this minute, but—"

"There's always a *but* isn't there?" *I want you because of who you are, not because of business.*

"But you're not thinking clearly because of the pharmaceuticals." He knelt in front of her and placed his hands on each side of her, his fingers grazing her thighs. "I'm going to find a shirt for you to wear, get you a glass of water, and then I'll sleep with you."

He touched me and has changed his mind. He desires me as much as I do him. Her head shot up, and her eyes widened. She licked her lips. His soft warm fingers touched her exposed skin, holding her still.

"No, love, I'll rest beside you. When we have sex, when we make love, it'll be memorable—a life changing experience—and I want you to be totally involved."

She panted little breaths, thankful she had a towel to absorb the heat and the moisture. "I'll be—"

He stuck his fingers to her lips. "Please don't make his harder for me. I'll be using your shower as it is." He lowered his hand. "Now, where are your nightclothes?"

She sighed. At least he'd be there, beside her all night.

"Top drawer, right side of the dresser." She pointed to her left.

He braced his hands on his knees and slowly rose. Within seconds she was out of the wet towel and into a silk nightgown. No lingering touches or glances. He was an honorable man. A man worthy of her love.

****

Stein wanted to feel the pain of the shards of water beating into his skin. He admitted one of the most difficult hurdles in his life thus far was not grabbing the opportunity to make love to her when she offered it. He yearned for her, and his cock could vouch for that.

He had considered Jessica's words, during the cab ride to Jeff Wanamaker and then to Kerry's house. Kerry needed the business deal to secure her CEO position. Why? If she was the sole survivor of old man McClure she should be a shoe-in. Tomorrow he'd ask about it, something was out of sync.

Each time he thought he had her categorized and stowed away into a tidy little pigeon-hole, she surprised him. She had so many different facets to her character: seductive, fierce, strong, sexy, and vulnerable.

Stein wrapped a towel around his waist and walked into the bedroom. She lay on her side, soft little breaths expelling out of her open mouth. He was thankful she'd finally crashed. Frustrated and horny as hell, he couldn't take any more of her temptations.

He smoothed the drying ringlets of hair from her face, and leaned over to kiss her cheek. He bumped the bedside table and her cell phone fell. As he bent to pick it up, he saw a stack of papers with his name boldly printed at the top. He pulled out the stack of fifty or more sheets. The phone lit as he placed it on top of the table.

"Stein," she murmured.

She remained asleep. Was she dreaming of him? He smiled and caressed her forehead. She wanted him as much as he wanted her. How he wanted her! So much it hurt to smell her womanly floral scent, and touch her soft skin.

Tomorrow, they would talk.

He picked up the stack of papers, walked around to the other side of the bed, removed the towel, and slid in beside her. He turned on the reading lamp and reviewed the copies of the emails he had sent to Kerry McClure when he'd thought her to be a male CEO. Rereading them, he noticed the change from normal business conversation to a softer and more personal tone. He had told Kerry about fishing in the freezing waters at his mountain retreat. A golf outing with Ian had a humorous anecdote. He gave her advice when she asked about office politics. By reading the missives, he acknowledged somewhere in his mind he had known Kerry McClure was a woman. Somehow he'd formed a connection with her, before he'd met her in person.

Stein placed the papers on the table, clicked off the light and rolled onto his side. He tucked his arm around her waist and inhaled her sweet scent. Sleep would be long in coming this night as his mind raced to review the events from the past few days. His cock reawakened with her fresh, supple skin rubbing against him. He rested until finally falling asleep as the sun peaked through the windows.

****

Kerry woke him with tiny, nibbling kisses up his neck to his cheek. She tasted mint from her toothpaste on his lips. The fresh scent wafted under her nose when she kissed him. She experienced the joy of being a seducer. The adrenaline rushed through her veins like she'd run a marathon. It would be easy to ignore the pain in her shoulder. All she had to do was convince him to make love to her. His rough fingers rested on her waist. She pushed her full naked breasts against his chest. Her leg slipped across his thighs, as she nestled against his pelvis. Her softness. His hardness.

"Stein." She kissed his lips. "It's a new day. I'm over the insane medicine. The pain's barely there.

Please, make me yours."

Please don't deny me. Her physical condition would not prevent her from achieving communion with this man. "Please, make me yours."

Kerry wanted him to be hers. The connection— inevitable.

She had raced for him like a horse to the finish line, and she had won. Now she could claim him. He would be hers. She gazed into his eyes, witnessed lust and acceptance.

He returned her kiss. The cherry scent from her lipstick heated. The shiny lip-gloss transferred onto his mouth, making it slick. She slowed the kiss, leaned into him, and touched the back of his head. He placed his hands on each side of her face, and added passion to the kiss. She moved and pulled gently at his lips. Vibrations from her moans must have stirred him, because his tongue explored her mouth intimately. The ache at her junction increased as his shaft grew larger.

The scent of her verbena bath soap on him tantalized her. Her breath came out in short pants. Did he feel the urgency? He moved and tightened his fingers at her rear. Because she cared for him, her first time would be memorable.

Kerry pushed her hands beside his head and situated herself firmly on top. Her mound brushed his stomach, the musky scent infiltrating the space. She rested her chest on top of his. His penis already full and tight rubbed against her.

His fingers stroked along the side of her face to the swell of her breasts. He stopped. Did he think her beautiful? Was he learning her silky contours? Her breasts filled his hand and throbbed. He leaned forward, drawing her flesh into his mouth, suckling firmly on the erect nipple.

She moaned.

He swirled his tongue around the other pearl

until its pink point budded and hardened. She needed more. She sat up, bringing her stomach within reach. He inhaled. Would he stop? *Please don't stop.*

His lips pressed against her abdomen. The roughness of his tongue tickled her as he made a circle around her navel. Her muscles tightened and the moisture collected between her thighs. The desire to experience more, to ease that ache vibrating between her thighs, urged her on.

She shoved him back, ran her fingers up one arm and raised it above his head. He latched onto the iron rail of the headboard, and she kissed the taut muscle bulging near his shoulder. She smiled and shifted on his lap working her pulsating vagina closer to the source of heat.

"Move your other arm up, so I can have unobstructed access to your fabulous body." She nibbled on his ear.

"Sweet Christ," he hissed as he shot his arm up and grabbed another white rail.

She leaned forward and dragged the tips of her rigid nipples down his chest. Her fingers stroked him, following the same path as her breasts. Her breasts separated and his penis slid between them. It pulsed. She lifted her glance to meet his gaze.

She spread her fingers around the head of his penis and pulled the thin bit of skin, gently with great care she shoved her mouth onto the head.

He sucked in his breath. His large hands clasped her head. She looked up and witnessed the pain in his eyes. Was she hurting him?

"Love." He took her arms into his hands and pulled her close, pressing his lips to hers. Careful of her injury, he eased her to the side and onto her back. "I don't want to hurt you."

She hugged him. An embrace with meaning, bodies tight, hands touching each other and breaths warming each other's skin.

"The only way you could possibly hurt me is if you pull away."

"Not likely to happen, love." He stroked his fingers against her skin. She was thankful he paid particular attention to the side of her breasts, and near her stomach. Goose bumps formed as he moved to caress the hairs at the apex of where she desired him to enter.

She pushed her hips upward. A musky scent filtered through the air. His finger slid inside her pulsating, wet vagina. Her muscles contracted adjusting to the invasion and pulled him further inside.

Stein thrust a second finger inside and within a few tweaks she moaned and twisted under his hand. Withdrawing his fingers, he straddled her, making sure to keep the bulk of his weight off of her shoulder. He kissed her, savoring the connection, and thrust inside her warm cavern.

"Oh, yes." She tensed, gasped, and dug her nails into his back.

He shifted, pulled back and stared into her brown eyes. They were passion filled. Her flushed cheeks drew his attention away from her swollen red lips.

A virgin. She was an innocent, with an experienced lover's instinct.

She deserved the utmost care, and he'd give her an orgasm. He'd satisfy her. He wanted to make her first time memorable, exciting, and fulfilling. From what he had read, the woman's first time wasn't always climatic, but he'd try his damnedest to give her one.

"Why didn't you tell me?"

"It's not important. We were meant to be together. Please, don't stop."

He withdrew, touched her clit, and massaged it

until she wiggled under him. A kiss to her right breast sent a moan from her luscious lips. He moved to her mouth while continuing to touch her erogenous zones—behind her knee, the soft white skin of her inner thigh, and the pulse points at her wrists.

"Now," she panted. "Please, I need you."

He reentered her tight wet space, breaking through the barrier. She held onto his back and lifted her hips. Her fingernails bit into his skin. He paused, letting her adjust to the invasion. She hissed out little breaths, and licked her lips. He kissed her, sucking in the taste of her, making love to her mouth, simultaneous with her vagina.

She twisted side to side, and pressed her entire body closer to him. They rocked in a timed rhythm. Her muscles tightened and cum clung to his cock as she screamed out her release.

Yes, she was his. He claimed her and soon she would realize they were meant to be together. He kissed the side of her cheek, inhaling the scent of his woman.

Her contractions pulled his penis deeper within her and pulsed around him. He paused, letting her experience the ecstasy of their union. The quivers would run its course. She panted and grabbed his butt, holding tight. A few minutes later she moved, securing them in her tight glove. He thrust. One and then another until his release came, merging them as one.

His arms braced on each side of her, he lifted and kissed her tenderly. She leaned into his neck as he eased out and slid to the side. He pulled her against him and held her close, feeling her rapid heartbeat pound against his chest. Should he tell her he loved her?

Her quick little breaths patted the side of his neck. "I love the way the Irish start the day," she murmured into his ear.

"I love the way my American starts the day," he responded. She chuckled and her breasts vibrated against him.

"That was amazing," she whispered.

"You're amazing." He smiled and caressed the side of her face. He eased his fingers along her jawbone, finishing at her lower lip. "Do you want to spend the day in bed then?"

She kissed the palm of his hand. Her glance met his.

"Yes, lovely idea." She touched his chest, a gentle touch, as light as butterfly wings. His nipples peaked. He wanted her again, stronger now than when he met her in the elevator five days ago, when they played the gander and touch game.

He cupped her neck and their lips met. Her lips were firm and passionate and then soft and ardent. She gently dug her fingernails into his skin on his arm and agitated the floral soap scent.

Her cell phone rang, playing a version of "Eye of the Tiger". Kerry broke the kiss, reached over, and pressed the speakerphone button.

"Kerry McClure."

Stein ran the palm of his hand down her side and rested his fingers in the cute dimple below her waist. She cat-backed—pushing her breasts forward, her rear out, stomach taut.

"It's Uncle Michael. I heard about the incident at The Garden Center yesterday. A board meeting has been called."

Chapter Twelve

Kerry tensed and rolled to the side of the bed, wrapping the sheet around her as she went. She snatched the phone off the table and tossed the trailing cloth like a wedding train over her forearm. White-hot-pain sliced through her shoulder.

A quick glance at Stein, she mouthed. "I'll be back." She walked out of the room.

She anticipated problems from her uncle as a result of getting injured while at The Garden Center, However, his voice held a joyful, gotcha, quality. She wouldn't allow him to spoil her first bit of happiness in over eleven months.

The shoulder pain made her nauseous. She forced the contents down and shuffled down the hallway.

"I'm contesting the decision of the board to appoint you as CEO," Mike stated bluntly.

So they had decided to appoint her. A smidgen of joy rushed through her.

"I don't understand your reason to take this action. I superseded my goals. My accomplishments will benefit McClure Ventures." She got a glass from the kitchen cabinet and shoved it against the refrigerator water dispenser. Her shoulder burned more and more with each move. Her stomach twisted with each word he spewed from his jealous lips.

Her heart had a stinging fire around it. She put the glass down and grabbed her chest. What did women feel when they experienced a heart attack?

She took the plastic container filled with over-the-counter pain relievers to the end of the counter top. She held the phone against her cheek and shoulder and attempted to open the vial. The blazing sharp pricks and pinching made her feel faint, but she refused to have the woozy feeling from the prescription drugs again today.

Stein took the bottle from her and opened the container. He slid two onto the lid and held it out to her. Thankful for his kindness and help, she glanced at him. His piercing blues held concern and a hint of annoyance. Anger at the caller or her?

"One of the staff members of McClure Ventures told me they overheard you making a deal with the CEO of Rune Technology? You exchanged sex for the agreement. Is this true? No, don't answer that because I'm sure it is. You're more like your mother everyday. You'll do whatever to get what you want."

Tears threatened to expose how much his harsh words hurt her. His brash comment of her could be ignored, but not the slanderous remark about her mother. She threw two tablets into her mouth and washed them down with water. She wiped her eyes with the edge of the sheet. *Inhale. Exhale. Get Control.*

"You can believe whatever fantasy you want Uncle Mike. I'm not going to explain my personal life to you. I've never exchanged sex for a business agreement. If you want to contest the appointment, do, but I warn you, I'll win and as permanent CEO your days will be numbered. Consider carefully before you become a distinguished absentee board member with no involvement." She tightened her grip on the sheet.

"I'll see you on Monday. Bring a packing box." He hung up.

With jittery hands she disconnected and mopped her brow. Darn, it wasn't over and going up against her uncle terrified her. He was older, sly, and persuasive. Could she win a battle against him?

Stein's hand slid around her waist. With gentleness, he tenderly shifted her close to his front. Was this how all lovers acted around each other? Her heart warmed with a rush of love—she hoped.

"Do you want to talk about it?"

She rested her head on his chest, grateful he had appeared in her life. Her shoulder burned and now her head hurt. But she didn't want to think, she only wanted to be coddled by the man supporting her.

"How much did you overhear?" The water rumbled inside her stomach.

"All of your side of the conversation." He carried her to the kitchen nook and sat down on a bench resting beneath the window. She snuggled onto his lap.

"How sweet! I've only seen this done in the movies. You're my hero," her voice came out scratchy, she coughed to clear it.

"Here's what I gathered. Your uncle wants the CEO position. You were appointed. He had an informant listen to our conversation yesterday, or someone happened to overhear. He believes you exchanged sexual favors in order to get the business deal. How am I doing?"

"Right on the money."

"I have a solution. Would you like to hear it?"

"Sure, why not." Her sinuses were clogged with unshed tears. She sounded as if she had a cold—a red nosed, pink-eyed, soporiferous cold. It continued to amaze her how unattractive she felt around this man. First the elevator escapade, then dressed as a stinky old man, and hot and sweaty yesterday at The Garden Center, topped off by an injured, weeping sap. She gathered her fortitude by straightening her spine, she would not show weakness. She'd be strong. Besides, what could happen next?

"We could say in Vegas we fell instantly in love. We had a squabble. If Wanamaker asks, we'll say you wanted to prove a point to me about a man conducting a meeting versus a woman. So you dressed like a moth-ridden old guy instead of being yourself and the point was made. Jessica and Ian will stand by us." He shifted her on his lap and outlined the quarter burn on her neck. Her chin automatically hit her chest, trying to hide the burn—her mark of dishonesty. "I of course recognized the gorgeous woman beneath."

She half-smiled. "I think that sounds plausible and close to the truth. But, I've done enough deception. I couldn't lie."

"It wouldn't be a lie from me. For the past two months I've been happy. Without realizing it, I had been romancing Kerry McClure. You give me pleasure." He lifted his eyebrows in that comical quick up and down motion he'd done before.

"I've been happy, too," she responded, trying to control the urge to shed her sheet and remove his jeans. Pleasure and pain were so very close.

"To validate this, I think we should fly back to Las Vegas and get married."

"I'm sorry. It sounded like you said we should get married." What was he thinking? Could she get married? It would be eternal. Should she tell him it would be forever and according to her beliefs, her religion, divorce wasn't an option?

"I did. Will you marry me?" With two fingers he tilted her head and their gazes locked. "What better way to validate the alibi? We'll tell them we quarreled, resolved our differences, and got married."

The man was insane, but her heart beat a quick rhythm at his suggestion. Her heart wanted to believe his invitation was a result of love, but they'd just met a few days ago, less than a week actually. Did he consider the emails a method of romance? She'd go back through them and see if any subtle hints indicated he knew she was a woman.

"I can't marry you. I don't know you."

"Love, you know me better than anyone. I've never spent more than a few seconds on an email until I started writing to you. Through messages, I unloaded my personal thoughts, described heritage, and my ambitions. I feel closer to you than I have any woman who has ever entered my life. Be my wife. Share a future with me." He entwined her fingers with his.

Her heart swelled with emotion. Part of her wanted to scream out, *'yes, I'll marry you'* but the logical part blocked the love she experienced and reinforced her declaration they were virtual strangers. She needed more time.

"For now, I'll share the hot tub with you. Are you interested?"

He sighed. "I don't have a suit with me." He kissed her neck at the pulse point.

"You don't need one. Well, maybe a raincoat."

****

Faith: believing in something without a guarantee.

Stein read the words over and over on the artwork in the bedroom, the colors of gold, red, green and white standing out on the blue sky. He had faith in destiny and knew without a doubt Kerry would come around. His mum always claimed he had a bit of magic in him. This was the very first time in his life he hoped that belief held true.

He and Kerry were meant to be together. Ironic, since he was more analytical than most. Yet he was willing to risk everything. Risk his future goals. Risk taking on a new paradigm by marrying someone he hardly knew, but someone he loved. Stein sought the change. He wanted to be the wizard to her gypsy.

She came out of the dressing room stuffing a brush and handkerchief into a purse. "What do you want to do next?"

"Trade in my Hanged Man card for a new one?" He smiled.

She chuckled. "Later," she winked, "we'll play cards."

His dick went full mast. "Shouldn't you be resting the shoulder?"

He met her in the middle of the room. The unmade bed with its maroon and gold striped sheets was stark against the pale walls. A rosary, the pearl beads wrapped in a circle with an onyx cross dangled over the edge of the bedside table, a bottle of water and pills were scattered across the surface.

Stein had a sudden and inexpiable desire to refuse to leave this quiet, comfortable room. If they went out in public, would their happiness end? Was their joining and impromptu relationship enough to survive judgment by outsiders or even family for that matter?

"I want to learn everything about you, so let's order food and stay here today." He pushed a strand of hair from underneath the sling strap and caressed the side of her neck.

"You know more about me than any other male alive." She hoisted the purse onto her good shoulder, took his hand into hers, and tugged him toward the door. "Come on. I need to get a breath of fresh air. We'll go to a restaurant for lunch and come right back. You can drive, right?"

"On the opposite side of the street, sure. Will you promise to tell me of your family, favorite color, food, band—"

"I get the idea. We'll trade information." She lifted onto her tiptoes and kissed his mouth. No dangerously tall heels graced her feet today.

He gave in to the power which had existed since Adam and Eve and kissed her back. He wrapped his arms around her tight, perfect-shaped rear and cradled her.

"You're insatiable," she whispered into his ear as she nipped at the lobe.

"Only with you, love." His cock was fully engorged just by having her near to him. He couldn't let her go. His stomach growled. "Right, then, down to the pub and back, because I want to keep you all to myself today."

"I adore your sense of possessiveness." She licked his bottom lip and kissed him with enough passion to cause his penis to press painfully against his jeans.

"How hungry are you?" His voice held a great deal of his homeland accent. He'd been trying for years to make his voice, and his words universal, but with Kerry he could be himself.

Her eyes fired with excitement, passion, and desire. She lowered the purse from her shoulder and reached out to him. His gaze left hers, only because of the horrible fog horn sound ringing through the room.

"What is that obnoxious noise?"

"The doorbell, but whoever is standing on the other side will leave." She slipped off her shoes. She fit beneath his chin. Her mouth touched the apex of his neck. His heart went pit-a-pat at a rate much higher than the dong, dong, dong.

"It's not going to stop. Answer the door and later I'll slowly undress you."

"Sounds like a fair trade to me," she said and pulled him with her to the front door.

"Let me open the damn thing, its heavy." Stein tugged the solid oak to reveal the nervous young man from yesterday.

He stood on the stoop with an envelope in his hand. His eyes widened, narrowed and his young mouth pinched into a disapproving frown. "I need to speak to Ms. McClure please."

Kerry popped her head around Stein. Bobby's eye nervously twitched. It jerked when she interviewed him and then again yesterday. Why was he anxious? His winker batted as fast as popcorn in a microwave.

"Kerry, may I speak to you, alone please?" Bobby rocked from foot to foot.

"Bobby, this is my friend, Stein Laxdale. Stein, this is my intern, Bobby Smith."

Stein held out his hand, and Bobby gave him a quick handshake.

Bobby stepped back and repeated the request. "I need to speak to you alone."

"Whatever you have to say to me, you can tell me in front of Stein."

Bobby glanced with his non-twitching eye, toward Stein and walked inside the foyer. Kerry didn't have a good feeling about whatever Bobby planned to announce.

"I'll step back and give the two of you a bit of privacy," Stein said.

Kerry turned to tell him no, but instead faced Bobby. "Why aren't you at the Center?"

"I'm sorry. You gave me a chance to work in a Fortune Five Hundred company, and I let you down." Bobby pushed the envelope toward her.

"What did you do?" She grasped the envelope and flipped it over to remove the contents. Nervously she bit down on her lower lip.

"I told your uncle the conversation you had with that man," he nodded at Stein, "yesterday." Bobby's eye was ready to spasm off his face.

"I don't understand why you didn't have faith in me. You listened to a conversation without knowing all of the details and instead of talking to me, you gave that limited information to my uncle. Why? Why would you?"

"He asked me questions. Wanted to know why I took you to the Emergency Room. Wanted to know what happened before you pulled your shoulder muscle. The man doesn't know how to take no for an answer." Bobby stuffed his shaking hands into his pants pockets and lowered his hazel eyes. "I let you down. If you want to fire me, I understand completely."

"I'm not going to fire you over this, but I might *can* you if you don't get to The Garden Center and make sure everything runs smoothly today." Bobby was a mere kid in a subordinate role, she could forgive him. But would the board see her viewpoint and accept her as a capable woman and CEO.

His face brightened, and he threw out a hand towards her. "I won't... I won't let you down again. I promise."

She shook his hand. "You'd better not. Most of the time in business, you don't get a second chance. Now, get to work."

Bobby pivoted, opened the door, and took off at a run for his car.

"Well done. I can see why your uncle is afraid of having you as CEO," Stein said.

"Those are fine words coming from a man who is up and coming in the technology field." She squinted at him. "Do you think my uncle is afraid? Is that the reason he continues to create problems for me?"

"No doubt about it, love."

Stein went from simple hero to white knight status, and she planned to be his damsel in distress. She wrapped an arm around his waist and threw the papers to the sofa. They scattered over the surface. One stood out strong and dark against the others. Kerry picked it up and scanned the words. Her joy plummeted. In the back of her mind, she hoped her uncle had been bluffing. He hadn't been.

"What is it?" Stein asked.

"All of the board members have signed a petition to consider revoking my appointment. A meeting will be held at nine Monday morning to discuss the situation."

"Doesn't seem logical. How many shares do you hold?"

"Fifty percent. My uncle has twenty and the remainder is scattered among three other board members."

"Then you have the deciding vote." Stein moved a curl of hair from around her chin and tucked it behind her ear.

"Normally, that would be the case. In this situation, my father had a codicil to his will stating until I was thirty years of age I had to be voted into the CEO position. I've five years to go." She dropped the page and it floated down to the sofa. Kerry resented the addendum. Her father should have trusted her. He should have known she'd take care of the company. Her chosen path had deviated, but she knew all aspects of the business ventures. She'd studied business and marketing at the university. Why hadn't her dad awarded her straight guardianship?

"Is your offer of marriage still on the table?" she asked with excitement.

"Yes. Although I'm surprised about the turn of topic, I knew you'd come around." He kissed her lips. She broke the kiss.

"I only know of two states which will marry an adult couple without a three day wait, Tennessee or Nevada? Tennessee is an hour flight, or about four hours to Vegas." Kerry dragged her cell phone out of her handbag, ready to dial at his okay. The solution, while unbelievable, met her desire to be with him.

Maybe theirs would eventually be a marriage with love.

"Since we met in Vegas, if we travel back there it'll appear as if we had planned it all along. It has so many fond memories for me, doesn't it for you?" His eyes twinkled with humor.

"Eight hours flying time, when do you have to be back in Ireland?"

"Certainly not until after the honeymoon." He winked. "Ian and I took an extra week for holiday. We've plenty of time. The meeting is Monday. We could stay over for one night in Vegas. Do you want me to see if the honeymoon suite is available at the *Yellow Fever*?"

"Yes," she chuckled at how insane she'd become. "The honeymoon suite will be a lovely idea. I'll call and get the McClure Ventures jet fueled and ready for take off. I'm going to ask Jessica to go along as my bridesmaid. Can you be ready to leave in two hours?"

"Yes, and I'll ask Ian to be my best man." He rubbed her back. "Don't worry, love, it'll all work out fine. Have faith."

Chapter Thirteen

The afternoon sun glinted off the side of the plane. The sound of other craft taking off added a cadence in the background. Kerry moved her sunglasses to rest on top of her head and wrapped her arm around the aging man's waist. "Jimbo, this is my fiancé, Stein Laxdale, his friend, Ian Johnston, and of course you know Jessica. Guys, meet the best pilot this side of the Atlantic, Mr. James Bow."

Jimbo's face flushed red, the stain creeping up to meet white and gray hair.

"She only said that because I let her play with the controls when she was a tiny little thing," he declared, blue eyes twinkling.

"She's what, five inches taller now? How do you reach the pedals of your car, Kerry?" Ian asked, with a devil-may-care grin on his handsome face.

Jimbo chuckled. "You boys are a might tall." He looked skyward. "My wife was Irish, bless her soul, and I truly miss the accent." A tear glinted in his eye.

"I'm sure after the four hour flight, you'll regret saying that to Ian. He loves to talk," Stein said.

"There's nothing like a good Irish tale," Jimbo said. "How long will you be in Vegas this time, Kerry?"

"Just overnight. Stein and I are getting married." She reached over and wove her fingers with Stein's.

"Saints be praised, never thought I'd live to see the day. Congratulations! Climb aboard then, and we'll be on our way." He took a piece of luggage and stowed it into the underbelly of the Gulfstream.

"Jimbo, would you step in for my father?" Her heart vibrated against her chest while she waited for his answer. Bold gestures weren't a part of her nature, but she wanted him to be her surrogate father. He and Jessica were her only true family members now.

He stopped mid-stride and lowered the travel bag to the concrete runway. He turned towards her and with an unsteady hand reached up to scratch his nose. "Kerry, I'd be right honored to escort you down the aisle."

She dropped Stein's hand and hugged the tall, lanky man. Her own little family would be there when she committed the rest of her life to Stein Laxdale.

"All right, then, let's get this buggy in the air." Jimbo patted her arm, shoved the bags into the craft and smiled as bright as Ruby Walsh when he brought Hedgehunt over the finish line at the Welsh National horse race. They'd had a wonderful time watching the race and sharing stories of her dad and his love of gambling. Now Jimbo would help her with a life-altering gamble. The race had started.

An hour later, in a hazy, happy state, Kerry observed her friends. Jessica relaxed on the sofa, her eyes closed as soft little wheezes came from her nose. Was she avoiding conversation with them? Kerry needed to have a heart-to-heart with her concerning her entanglement with Ian. Stein and Ian were deep into a conversation regarding a storage solution for a company exporting fish.

Stein conversed with an innate noble quality. She loved the way his hands moved—fluid, yet with precision. He leaned forward when he wanted to make a point very clear, or if he was intently interested in what was being said. His blue polo shirt, stretched tight against his back, defined the strong muscles underneath. When he was excited his eyes glowed with an inner joy, and they narrowed when he questioned or prepared to disagree.

Yes, she had fallen for this man, but was she doing the right thing? Marriage should be based on love not lust. Certainly, she should not marry because she wanted to secure the top spot in her company. Did she love him?

"What are you thinking? You frowned and now you've a soft smile on your face. You look so relaxed." He kissed her cheek and whispered into her ear. "Did you take a muscle-relaxer?"

She shook her head and kissed his lips. "No. I want to be able to walk straight down the aisle without a tilt." Kerry rose from the upholstered green chair. Stein sat down, clasped onto her wrist and pulled her onto his lap. She settled in and traced the dark azure blue Rune symbol S on his left breast, Rune Technology's business logo.

"Is that a bedroom through the door straight ahead?" He nodded toward one of the two doors, and then nibbled on her neck.

She nodded, breathing unsteady, her heart pounding as fast as the tap-tap-tap of Ian's fingers on the keyboard.

"Do we have time to use it?"

She shook her head. "Maybe on the way back." She tucked her head between his chin and shoulder.

"Are you in pain? It's been several hours since you took the ibuprofen." He rubbed his jaw on the top of her head and made tiny circles with his fingers along the side of her arm.

"Not bad. I'll wait until after the ceremony, and then take some aspirin or something. Stein..." she whispered, while glancing over at Ian and Jessica to see if they were listening. They were involved in their own animated conversation. Jessica jetted out of her seat and went into the pilot's cabin, sitting down beside Jimbo.

"Yes, love."

"You don't have to do this. There's time to change your mind. We could go and just have a good time."

"Have you changed your mind then, Kerry?" His voice held a hint of anger and something else. A tone she couldn't define, reestablishing the fact she didn't know him well enough.

"No, I haven't. You're in for the gamble of your life, Mr. Laxdale."

"I don't believe I'll lose this one, Ms. McClure. I'll have won the half-million."

Her head shot up and her gaze connected with his. His smile was stretched across his face and reflected in his dreamy blue eyes. At that point in time, Kerry felt like the half-million dollar prize.

"Why am I not a million?" she queried. Contrary to the joy she had zinging through her body, she tried to force her mouth to form into a frown.

"Because you're a little tiny thang." Stein imitated Jimbo's southern Indiana accent exactly.

She chuckled. "We're going to have a good marriage, a good partnership, aren't we, Stein?" *Tell me yes. Make me feel like I'm doing the right thing and not gambling with your future.*

"You can bet on it, future Mrs. Kerry Laxdale."

"Mrs. Kerry Laxdale. It has a ring, doesn't it?"

"Lucky me, I get a CEO, a fortuneteller, and a sexy little diva bundled in one package."

"Maybe we do have time to use the bedroom," she whispered and sucked on his lower lip.

"Ten minutes until we land at McCarran Airport. You kids get seat-belted up," Jimbo announced over the intercom. Jessica rejoined them in the cabin.

"Damn." Stein shifted in the seat.

"Exactly." Kerry rose from his lap and sat in the chair beside his, hugging her arm close to her chest.

"Jessica, was Ramon able to arrange a priest?" Kerry fidgeted with the scarf tied around her neck hiding the burn mark.

"Yes, one of his friends will meet us for the ceremony in two hours. We'll have enough time to unload our stuff at the hotel and change. Your library friend, Mrs. Martinez is sending over a limo to take us straight there and the driver will be at our disposal the remainder of the night." Jessica glanced over at Stein.

Kerry knew, despite Jessica's monologue in the hotel room a few days ago, she wasn't in favor of their quickie marriage.

"What is your affiliation with the library, Kerry? I never connected the two," Stein asked.

"My mother worked at the Las Vegas Library on the boulevard. My father and a buddy walked in looking for the Clark County Law Library on Third Street. A spark of love appeared and my mother, Marlee Russell, was lost in the flame of Conner McClure. They were married for thirty years before my mother was killed in a car accident. Eleven months ago my father died of a massive heart attack."

"So, you've lost both parents." He leaned forward and speared her with a sympathetic gaze.

"Yes. In my mother's memory, I support the library in whatever way possible."

"I'm thankful for that and that little gypsy outfit you wore the day in the elevator."

She hated the heat as it rose to her face, reminding her they weren't alone in the cabin.

Stein grinned. "I'm even more thankful for the pharmaceutical which relaxed you so much you let me into your home, bed, and heart."

"Seriously, for a man who proclaims to rarely

talk, you're getting a lot of information out there," Kerry said, pasting on saccharine smile.

Ian chuckled. Jessica's eyes narrowed and her mouth formed a tight line. She slammed her fist into his arm with enough force to tilt him like a punching clown. Jessica would always be her champion. Kerry pursed her lips. Jessica might have used the comment and Ian's reaction to punch him like a pre-teen punches a boy she likes.

The tires of the silver bird smoothly connected with the concrete as Jimbo brought the plane to a complete stop. He opened the cabin door, letting the warm early evening air flood the interior. The airport staff lowered the steps and helped unload the luggage.

"Kerry, Jessica gave me all of the details, so I'll take care of the plane and meet you at the wedding." Jimbo said, as he grabbed the railing to ascend the steps into the plane.

"Thank you, Jimbo. It means a lot to me to have you there."

He gave a quick nod and disappeared into the cabin. Stein assisted her inside the black car, while Jessica talked to the suave chauffeur. The man, dressed totally in black, had sleek brown hair and a winsome smile. He helped Jessica inside the dark limo, and within seconds, they were en route to the hotel twenty minutes away.

Kerry's stomach rumbled with queasiness. The salad she'd eaten six hours ago rushed up and settled down, unable to find a balance. She crossed her arms at her waist. "How many rooms did you get, Stein?" she asked.

Stein glanced over at Ian. "How many rooms did you get?"

Ian's glance shot over to Jessica. The fear in his eyes made Kerry want to laugh. Why did he ask Jessica to arrange rooms if they were on the outs?

"How many rooms did you get, Jessica?" His voice held a tinge of anger.

"I obtained three rooms, one for you lovebirds and one for each of us." She gave Ian a lopsided, snarky smile. "I charged Rune Technology, since the Euro is higher than the USD at this time."

Kerry chuckled, knowing this was Jessica's way of testing Stein. How he reacted to the announcement would put him in the plus or negative category.

"Were you able to get the honeymoon suite?" He held Kerry's hand, slowly rubbing his thumb along the palm.

"Yes, our rooms are two floors below yours. Kerry, we'll use my room for you to change."

"I'll use Ian's room instead, so Kerry won't have to move her luggage again. If that's okay with you?" Stein asked.

Jessica nodded.

Kerry smiled. One point for chivalry. She glanced over to see Ian's half-lidded eyes. His tight jaw made his face appear thinner and angry. Jessica said they didn't fit. Could it be they really do fit, but she wasn't admitting it?

"How did your date go last night?" Kerry asked.

Jessica's back became ramrod straight.

"Not as well as I expected. We'll talk about it, later," Jessica answered, her voice as cold as the air coming from the vent beside Kerry's face.

This being said, in conjunction with the don't-talk-about-it glare, Kerry closed her mouth.

Ian opened his PDA and punched buttons as if they were stuck. Kerry shot her glance back to Jessica.

"Don't say anything else," Jessica mouthed.

Kerry gave a slight nod. "What's the name of the church again?"

"Garden something. We have a driver to get us

there." Jessica answered and crossed her slim long legs, drawing Ian's gaze. *The tease.*

Within seconds, the vehicle glided into the circular driveway of the hotel. An attendant helped Kerry out of the car. "Welcome to *Yellow Fever.* Please enjoy your stay."

The chauffer assisted Jessica out from the other side. Stein climbed out next.

"I'll be waiting for you here in one hour, right?" the chauffer asked, while holding Jessica's hand a little too long to be considered proper.

"Yes, thank you, Cameron." Jessica batted her eyelashes at the obviously interested fellow.

Kerry arched an eyebrow. *What's up with this little drama?*

Ian shoved his long legs out of the car, slamming the rear passenger door into Jessica's backside, throwing her into Cameron's arms. Kerry kept her gaze on Ian, who grimaced and shot upward between the two.

"Sorry, love, clumsy big feet. Are you all right, then?" He ran his hand down Jessica's side and spent a few minutes rubbing a circular pattern on her rear where the door had bumped.

"Release me," she growled and pushed his hand away.

Kerry snickered until all three looked at her. She quickly turned it into a cough and plunged her hand inside her handbag to dig around.

"Come along, Kerry. I'll see you to the room." Stein flagged a bellhop to get their limited luggage. He cupped her elbow and escorted her into the lobby.

"What was that all about?" She leaned into Stein. The pills had worn off and her shoulder hurt like a thousand little miners pounded on each muscle.

"It's between the two of them. I'm goin' to let you rest here, while I get the keys to the rooms." She sat in the gold Queen Anne chair with as much grace as she could muster given the amount of pain.

Through the grand lobby doors, she could see Jessica and Ian arguing. The limo had left and the doorman looked over their heads. The two had a tough way to go if their relationship started with arguments. Of course, she didn't have the right to judge, her inciting moment with Stein was not stellar.

Kerry held her arm close to her chest. Should she try to give Stein another chance to back out? They would have the business deal regardless if they were married or not. If he didn't back out, would she always wonder if it was because of the situation, gallantry, virginity and all, or dare she hope that he loved her?

"Come along, love. There isn't much time until we should be at the ceremony." He helped her to her feet and turned as Jessica and Ian stomped through the doors.

"Jessica, here is the keycard to room 2537. I hope you'll have my bride in the lobby in forty-five minutes." Stein handed over the plastic keys. Concern and sadness etched across Jessica's face. Kerry questioned the interactions between Jessica and Ian.

"No problem, Stein. We'll be here in white and gold." She grabbed Kerry's good arm and escorted her to the elevator. The bellhop followed meekly, almost running to keep up with Jessica's swift step.

"Wait, I wanted to talk to Stein," Kerry said. She pivoted. He and Ian were in a heated discussion, toe-to-toe. Ian's hands clenched, knuckles tight against his hips. Stein's hands were tucked into his jean pockets, but his head was tilted to the side and his jaw hardened. The man was pissed, and not in the Irish way.

"You'll see him in a few minutes. We need to get

to the honeymoon suite. Your hair needs to be arranged and clothes changed." Jessica stepped into the elevator and pushed the button to take them to the twenty-fifth floor.

"I need to figure out if I can take a pain pill. Did we pack them? Do you think I can cut one in half?"

Jessica rubbed Kerry's back. Kerry snuck a peek at the bellhop to see if he listened. His stare remained fixed on the elevator doors.

"Do we need to talk about what will happen tonight? Too bad you've hurt your shoulder, so near the great sexcapade." Jessica's voice came out schoolmarm perfect, ready to teach the uneducated.

"Um-hum." Kerry searched through her large black purse seeking the tiny pain relieving pills.

"You've already had sex with him, haven't you?" Jessica asked, or accused. Her tone was biting as if the joy had been snatched from her.

Kerry glanced at her, while her fingers continued to search for the bottle. Jessica's eyes widened, glinting with humor, she put two fingers in front of her mouth as if in horror.

Kerry shot a frown at her friend and nodded toward the bellhop, who didn't blink. Out from her handbag flew the bottle of pills. Jessica bent down and picked up the container.

"When did this happen?" She handed the pills over.

"Early this morning." Kerry whispered and gave her a cheeky grin as she clasped the bottle tight in her fist.

"Good enough that you want to marry him?"

"That's why I'm here." She tried to keep her voice firm and confident, when she continued to question herself about the marriage. Should she? Should she not?

"I thought you were here because you love him."

"Jess, you know why you're my best friend?"

"Yes, because no one else can read your thoughts, which saves you a great deal of talking time. Ironic since you love to talk."

"You're my best friend because you know me so well. Nice to know how you feel about my verbal skills though." Kerry tried to twist the cap on the bottle.

The elevator doors opened, and a few steps later they arrived at the honeymoon suite. A quick swipe of the plastic key and Jessica threw the door open.

The bellhop placed the luggage inside and Jessica slipped him a five and a wink. Kerry, embarrassed about the conversation he had to have overheard, tried to tell herself it was Vegas. He'd probably heard more graphic things than that, seen more explicit situations.

Jessica made a three-sixty turn. "Crap, its beautiful and you only get it for one night."

Kerry had to agree. An entire wall of windows overlooked The Strip. The lights were beginning to shine in the darkening sky. The glitter and garish glamour never appealed to her, until now. She was seeing it from a different viewpoint. Her outlook on life had changed as she took new roles. She was a partner and a lover. Love. She loved Stein, a man she'd known for only a few days; yet, for a lifetime.

"As much as I want to plop down on that decadent white, suede couch I know we have a limited time frame to work in. Go shower and then we'll get you dressed and your hair arranged. Do you need help getting the shirt off?"

"No. I think I'll be fine." Kerry got the bottle open and dumped the pills out onto the glass table top.

"Can you help me divide one of these pills."

"What about the champagne?"

"You're right." She emptied out her purse to locate the ibuprofen. Jessica placed a glass of water beside her. She popped the tablets into her mouth and washed them down.

"Maybe the shower will help. Put it on full blast and hot. It should relax the muscles a bit. I'm going down to my room and shower. I'll be back up in a few." She snapped the handle of her weekender and tugged it out the door.

Thirty minutes later, Jessica walked through the door. Kerry was almost ready to be dressed and primped. She'd placed the dryer in a basket, propped by towels, and leaned over it to dry her hair. She shut it off and ran her fingers through the wavy mass.

"How's it going?"

"Well. I feel much better. The hot shower worked. Help me with the gown, and I'll be good to go." She smiled and walked into the main room.

"Sit and I'll see what I can do to make your hair look festive."

Kerry sat in a barrel back chair in front of the windows overlooking Las Vegas.

Jessica, amazingly talented with hairstyles, had Kerry's hair fluffed and arranged in a Grecian knot within minutes. "I don't know why you put your hair in a clip all the time. It has a lovely light brown color and the texture is perfect, not too thick, not too thin."

"Just right, huh?" Kerry winked.

Jessica rolled her eyes. "Come on, let's see how the dress looks."

Kerry rose from the chair, lifted the dress bag from the sofa, and removed the white silk confection. She took the garment off the hanger, opened the zipper, and stepped into the luxurious, pristine garment.

Jessica helped her tug the material into place and zipped the closure together. Kerry fastened the belt.

"I love the classic princess line, the belt makes your waist look like its fourteen inches. Good that it's sleeveless, so it won't pull on your shoulder. It's fabulous. You look beautiful." Jessica secured the clasp at the neck.

"Lucky I had it in the closet for a summer event. Who knew I'd be wearing it three months early." Kerry turned to gaze at her friend. "You decided to go with the royal blue instead of gold?"

"Yes, it's the same line as yours. Hopefully, they'll have a photographer."

"No worries, I packed a digital camera. We'll have Cameron take photos." Kerry squinted at her friend. "Are you going to tell me what's up with you and the driver, and you and Ian? I assume you went on a date last night with Ian?"

"We don't have time to go into it." Her lips tightened with a mutinous expression.

"Jess, I'm not leaving this room until you give me something."

"I've dated Cameron in the past—last year when we came out to give the library a big ol' check. I did go out with Ian. Again, we don't fit. He has an attitude and thinks one night of sex qualifies him to put rules on our relationship." A long drawn out sigh escaped. She busied her hands by placing the hanger back in the bag and slipped it on the closet doorknob.

"Uh, huh." Kerry repeated and followed Jessica's earlier uttering. "There's more," she insisted.

"Another time I'll tell you the rest, let's go." Jessica brushed off the edge of her dress. "Kerry, it's not too late to back out of this marriage."

"I'm not backing out. I want to be with him—everyday, for the rest of my life." Kerry picked up her slender white handbag. She stuffed lipstick, perfume, a shiny new penny, and a handkerchief inside. "I need something blue."

Jessica unpinned the flower from the waist of

her outfit and handed it over.

"Great, something borrowed and blue." She attempted to fasten it to the left shoulder. Her hand dropped as the muscles contracted and sharp pins of pain jetted through. The cloth flower fell to the floor.

Jessica picked up the flower. "Come here."

Kerry took a step forward and Jess fastened it to her shoulder.

She placed her hand on Kerry's forearm. "Don't you think you'd get the CEO position without going to the extreme of marrying this stranger?" Jessica's voice sounded strained.

Kerry took Jessica's hand into hers. "Yes, because I am my father's daughter. Neither the company, nor saving The Garden Center is my concern today. It's about Stein. I'm in love with him. I want to be with him. When I'm not with him I think of him. He makes me feel ... complete." Kerry met Jessica's gaze dead-on.

"Sounds like love." Her gentle smile turned into a frown. "Although, I'm not a fan of love or commitment, you are."

"Guess I'll find out if I am."

"Do you hear a knock?" Jessica asked.

Kerry nodded and glanced at the ornate rimmed wall clock, shaped like a gold nugget. "We're late."

Jessica's long legged stride got her to the door in seconds. She threw it open. Ian, hands on hips and elbows jutting out to the side. Emotion flittered across his eyes. *Worry and concern?*

Kerry's heart beat faster. She wiped her hands down her dress. Ian's lips tightened and a tick vibrated on his lower right cheek.

Chapter Fourteen

Please don't let him have changed his mind. Kerry rushed forward to grab Ian's arm, the silk dress rustling with each step she took. "Yes, what is it?"

"Stein's afraid you've changed your mind. Have you?" His gaze remained fixed on Jessica.

"No, we're just running late. We were on our way." Kerry sighed, a long expansive sigh, like after a difficult run. Stein thought the same thing she had. She smiled, snatched the keycard off the foyer table, and dumped it into her wallet size purse. The pain reliever finally kicked in.

Ian stepped back. Kerry breezed by him, then stopped and waited for them to catch up. She leaned against the elevator button and stared at them. Jessica took her sweet time gathering her purse and seductively swinging her hips over the threshold. Ian's tick grew more pronounced as the silence grew thick and weighty inside the elevator.

When the elevator doors opened into the lobby she saw her heart's desire. Dressed in an elegant black suit, he paced back and forth by the chair she had vacated only an hour before. Her heart clicked a beat as rapid as the alarms clinking on the slot machines. Yep, she had fallen in love with Stein Laxdale.

He looked up. She met his gaze, his frown became a smile and his eyes widened. He'd had every reason to be surprised. Stein had seen her in a variety of apparel from gypsy, to a man's suit, to grungy T's. For the first time she felt like an attractive woman. He started toward her and hesitated. Her heart beat stopped. Had he realized how little time they'd known each other? Had he changed his mind?

Stein rushed forward as Kerry walked out of the elevator, until his feet refused to move. He stood dead center under the massive glass chandelier. Stein's breath caught in his throat and he released it with a slow exhale. From the corner of his eye he saw gamblers and guests of the hotel and casino halt mid-stride. He knew they were staring at his fiancée, a dream in white. The dress highlighted her best features. A tiny belt around her waist, the length ending at the knees, showcased her sexy tanned legs. He took in her radiance as she closed the distance between them.

"Kerry, you're a vision of beauty. I'm the luckiest man in Vegas tonight." He leaned over and kissed her pink, shiny lips. He had feared she had changed her mind. She hadn't. She stood before him, a glittering brown-eyed wonder.

"And I'm the luckiest woman," she whispered against his lips, and then followed with a gentle kiss.

"I was wrong." He folded her into his arms. "You're a million."

He breathed in her floral scent to remember it and this moment for the rest of his life.

"Will you marry me, Kerry McClure?" *Love me, stay with me forever.*

"Yes, I'll marry you, Stein Laxdale."

He stepped back and linked her hand with his. They walked out of the air-conditioned hotel into the warm evening air, not really knowing where they were going. It didn't matter, because he'd won the lottery. He'd won the woman of his dreams. And he hoped she'd eventually love him.

The chauffeur held the door, and they settled

into the back seat of a long, black, stretch limo. She stared at Stein. He gazed into her eyes. Her twisted hair revealed her slender neck. Jessica said something from outside the car and Kerry leaned over him to look at her. The tiny pearl earrings bobbed as she moved her head, nodding to something Jessica said. A tear-shaped pearl hung at the end of a gold necklace snug against her throat. The burn must have been covered with makeup. An odd, large, blue flower looked out of place on her shoulder. He hadn't listened to her and Jessica's conversation, because like a gambler at the tables, he was totally addicted to Kerry McClure.

Stein moved his gaze from her throat, to her fathomless eyes. She arched an eyebrow. He inhaled deeply of her woman scent, took her hand in his and focused on Jessica and Ian, who remained outside the vehicle.

Stein overheard the driver tell Jessica she looked good enough to eat. Crass, some men just didn't have the right pick up line. He hoped Ian thought the same, or shortly he'd hear a fist connect with the driver's face.

Jessica stiffly slid onto the bench seat across from Stein, and Ian climbed in beside her. Through the open door the driver handed Jessica two bouquets. She handed a bundle to Kerry and placed a smaller posy in her own lap. The fresh floral scent of violets, roses, and lily-of-the-valley enveloped the car.

"Flowers, how sweet?" Kerry leaned over and kissed him, an inadequate nudge when he desired a full out passionate embrace.

He shifted in the seat. "I didn—"

"Good call on the flower choice, Stein," Jessica said and winked at him as Kerry lifted the bouquet to her nose.

"Thank you," Stein replied.

Five minutes later the driver passed by the Mirage. A fake volcano, erupting red, orange and blue fire into the night sky drew his gaze out the side window. The magnitude, the height and breath of the illusion amazed him.

"That's an illusion, right?" Ian asked.

"No, it's a simulation. The fire is real, which is why they have it so far away from people," the chauffeur said, through the privacy opening. He drove the car into an alley and parked in front of a wire fence that reached up into the sky at least twelve feet high.

"Oh, Jessica, you didn't," Kerry said. The expression on her face, like that of a child at Christmas, indicated she hoped Jessica had.

"Didn't what?" Stein asked.

"The Secret Garden?" Kerry had a catch in her throat. She released his hand and placed her palm on her heart.

"Your wedding day should be special."

Kerry lunged forward to hug her friend. They rocked back and forth.

"Will someone explain what the bloody hell is going on?" Stein asked.

Kerry sat back in the seat, a smile on her face. She held her arm close to her chest and wiped her eyes with her free hand. Her leg snug against his made him want to get the wedding over with and make love to her until the sun rose in the sky.

"The Secret Garden is a lush patch hidden in the inner core of the Mirage Hotel. It's in conjunction with a dolphin habitat and my favorite place to visit when I'm in Las Vegas. The only time I didn't visit was —"

"They've opened it up for special events, and your wedding should be special. My gift to you and Stein." Jessica met his stare and nodded.

"I'm amazed you were able to get it arranged in

just a few hours."

"A friend of a friend knows the special events manager."

Stein accepted the gift and the friendship Jessica implied. She wanted to make Kerry's wedding day special and memorable, so did he. They got out of the car and walked through the private entrance.

"Hell, my snow globe isn't going to compare to this gift," Ian said, as they strolled down the path with the dark green foliage and bright orange, yellow, blue, and red flowers sprinkled throughout.

"The globe will be close to my heart, Ian, because you chose it." Kerry clasped her purse and flowers close to her side and smiled at him.

She entwined her fingers with Stein's and suddenly stopped. There in the middle of the path, she tightened her grip. "Oh, how lovely."

Ian stepped aside.

Stein reluctantly lifted his gaze from his bride. The clearing had been decorated with tiny white lights glittering in the slight breeze, bright in the deep purple of the evening. A gazebo, with a mosquito net covering tied to the posts, remained simple and unadorned. A pale, diminutive man clothed in black priest's vestments stood in the middle of the platform.

A crowning or wedding was generally a formal event, so he rejoiced in having a man of God provide the matrimonial ceremony. The cleric privileged them with his appearance and currently stood in the center of the gazebo holding a brown leather book. At least twenty guests rose from their chairs. Kerry stopped and gasped.

"The volunteers and staff from the library," she whispered.

Jimbo, dressed in a black tux, trotted with a steady gait down the white cloth. The material had been laid on the ground and red rose petals were scattered throughout.

"Are you ready, Kerry?" Jimbo asked.

Kerry swung her gaze toward Stein. "Are you ready?"

"Since the minute I met you, love." He leaned down and kissed her. "I'll see you at the end."

Kerry nodded as her throat closed, choked off by unexpected tears of joy. In a few minutes she'd vow to take this man 'til death do they part and for her it would be a lovely journey getting to know the different facets of his character.

Stein and Ian skirted around the rose petals and went to stand on the gazebo platform beside the priest.

"Jessica, I don't know what to say. It's amazing. You're amazing." She hugged her friend. "Oops, don't want to bruise the flowers."

"I love you, and I know you'll only get married once. So I wanted it to be perfect, despite the reason for the rush." She grabbed her hand. "Are you ready to jump over the broom?"

"Yes. Let's get this ritual started."

Jessica turned to walk down the aisle. Kerry touched her arm, and Jessica tilted her head to look back.

"I love you, too."

Jessica smiled, grasped her flowers and strode down the white cloth runner, causing fragrant rose petals to rise from the surface and stir in the wind.

The wedding march came from nearby speakers. Kerry straightened her dress and situated the pocket size purse and flowers in front of her.

"Let's go," she said.

Jimbo patted her fingers. "Kerry, I know your father would have approved of Stein. He's a good guy."

She nodded, as tears cut off her vocal cords.

Jimbo held out his arm, and she clasped his elbow. Together they walked through nature's natural trellis toward the tiny bits of light in the clearing. Toward Stein.

Focused on the gazebo, she met his gaze. He smiled. One hand rested on top of the other, he lifted a finger. Her heart beat in rhythm to the song, as the thump of the march slowed, the fear inside her subsided. She exhaled and placed one cream-tinted, heeled foot forward, and then another step.

Her mother's friends, now her friends, stood as she walked by and smiled at her with tenderness in their eyes. The slight breeze didn't dry the tears that welled in her eyes.

Kerry kissed Jimbo on the cheek and glimpsed a tear shimmering in his eye. Stein lifted his arm to handfast with hers and help her step up to the platform. With unsteady knees she took her place beside Stein. He entwined her fingers with his. She gazed at him, and he winked. Like a flash of the volcano blasts in front of the Mirage, her heart sprung into her throat. She glanced into the now black sky, the twinkling stars providing a guiding light.

Thank you! How would it be possible to express her joy and gratitude? Her life had taken a sudden spin in a different direction, and she was unearthly happy.

She realized this union would be a good thing. They'd have a positive relationship, maybe share love someday, and if she was lucky, children as well.

"Good evening, Kerry and Stein. I'm Father Michael. Congratulations! Shall we begin?"

"Yes, Father," Kerry said. Stein nodded.

"Please be seated," the priest declared.

The clang of chairs and sighs were heard from behind her. Kerry remained straight-backed with her hands clutching the floral bouquet.

"Friends, family, guests, we are gathered here today to honor the love of Kerry Lynn McClure and Stein Aaron Laxdale. Marriage isn't something to enter into lightly, but a serious lifelong obligation to love, to have, to hold until death do you part."

Kerry listened as the man of the cloth recited poems of love and loyalty, honor and respect. His voice was deep and resonated into the night, even when his bald head bent to refer to passages in the Good Book. The man's black robe billowed when a breeze picked up, flapping against the white of Kerry's gown.

The words she'd heard at least a dozen times before were profound in their honesty. The ancient lyrical bits of wisdom held a different meaning for her now than in the past. Today the words bound her and Stein together. And for her, their marriage would be a lifetime commitment. Her fantasy had come true. Although, until now, she hadn't realized she had yearned for a man to have, to hold, and to love.

She relaxed. Stein's sandalwood scent mingled with the violets, roses, and lily-of-the-valley in her bouquet. He helped her lower to the kneeling bench at the appropriate times. She answered questions as required and was pleasantly surprised when he slipped a ring onto her finger.

"You may kiss the bride." The deep voice, coming from the surprisingly thin holy man, echoed off the gazebo's canvas ceiling.

Stein kissed her softly on her trembling lips. She relaxed and returned his kiss, giving as much as taking. He smiled against her lips when the crowd chuckled and coughed. Kerry broke away from him, lowered her head, and fumbled with the flowers.

He whispered into her ear, "Never be embarrassed about kissing me, Mrs. Laxdale."

She rested her forehead against his chest.

"Ladies and gentlemen, I'm proud to present Mr. and Mrs. Stein Laxdale."

Kerry gathered her courage, took Stein's arm, and promenaded down the rose petal-strewn runner.

Jessica slid beside Kerry at the end of the walk. "There wasn't enough time for catering a meal, but the Mirage Banquet did arrange a cake and champagne fountain. I was told Bernard Ibarra, Executive Chef, baked the cake himself."

"Why would he do that?" Kerry asked.

"He uses the library and has admiration for a woman who has found her true destiny." Jessica shrugged, as if that one little statement answered all the questions in the universe.

"Goodness! I'm so honored. I'll make a special effort to thank him." Kerry gave a thorough examination of the beautiful cake, magnificent in its simplicity.

Jessica took the bride's bouquet and purse as a string ensemble softly played in the background. "Go, celebrate your day!"

Kerry greeted the guests nearest to her. Stein joined her, but it wasn't long enough. A few minutes later Ian called Stein aside.

Jessica handed Kerry a drink of water. As she chatted about what Kerry might expect back in the bedroom, in bawdy terms, Kerry watched Stein move from group to group across the clearing.

There's my husband. I can't believe I took the leap.

Guests sipped clear bubbly while sitting at white-clothed tables. They were having fun. Joy flooded her as her husband glanced up from talking to Jimbo and smiled at her. His eyes crinkled at the corners, illuminating the tiny white lines the sun missed as it kissed his handsome face.

She had chosen a different route to follow, one totally diverse from her original scheme, and destiny brought her to this point. Friends, family, and a connection to someone, a love she intended to last a lifetime. The formula to a happy life, a higher peace, could only be found through love.

Ian mouthed something in their direction. Kerry glanced from him to Jessica, who huffed and whirled away. Kerry joined Stein and Jimbo in the front of the gazebo. Jimbo's smile spread wide and suddenly fell. Ava stalked toward their little group.

"Excuse me," Jimbo said and slid behind the gazebo.

"Hi, do you want to cut the cake and sip some champagne?" Kerry snuggled close to Stein's side and watched Ava change her course.

"Will it get us closer to the honeymoon?" He kissed her forehead and slid his arm around her waist.

"Most certainly." The excitement about their first union as man and wife made her tingle. She couldn't wait to experience their joining again. She ignored the twinges in her shoulder and focused on his lips. His fingers stroked her palm, making her yearn for him.

"Yes, we'll eat, drink, and soon be merry," he dryly answered and kissed her lips, creating a slow burn to connect with the twinge.

She giggled, like a teenager in love for the first time. "Come along then."

Kerry took his hand and together they sliced a piece from the two-tier cake. The sweet vanilla scent wafted through the air, tantalizing her. The wedding couple on top of the cake were old-fashioned in their uncomplicated elegance. As she and Stein fed each other a bite, a round of congratulations went through the group. The cake was delicious, even the second time when she licked it off his lips.

"It'll be awkward, but since your right shoulder pains you. We'll use opposite hands to entwine and drink from the cup of plenty," Stein whispered.

"How did you know the shoulder was bothering me?" she whispered back.

"Jessica told Ian, he told me, and I'll try not to spill the champagne all over your lovely dress."

"I've tried to not let it bother me. It's not life-altering." But, she was thankful when the celebratory drink went off without incident. Had others noticed her favoring one side?

However, marriage was life-altering.

The entire wedding must have been a shock to Stein, since he anticipated the priest, Ian and Jessica being the only witnesses. Instead, they had the entire library volunteer group. He never lost his calm demeanor or the pleasant smile on his face. She overheard him telling an off-color joke to Jimbo and Cameron. He praised Ava for getting Kerry's friends together. Her heart beat a quick, happy cadence when he animatedly talked and laughed with Jessica.

She glanced at her best friend. The sense of relief that Jessica accepted Stein made Kerry feel at ease and rejoice in the newfound fellowship of her fledgling family.

Kerry caught his sandalwood scent as his fingers grazed her arm. She leaned into him as he wrapped his arm across her hips.

"Tired, darlin'?" He placed his head against hers, his clean shaven cheek stroking her face.

"A little. It's all so overwhelming."

"You're happy then?"

"In spades." She turned and reached up to kiss him but parted as she heard a murmured word.

Ava stood in front of them. She hugged each of them. "Kerry, I'm a little disappointed you didn't choose my son, but I must admit you make a lovely couple." She pushed her index finger into Stein's chest. "I haven't seen Kerry this happy in years.

Treat her with care, Stein. She's a special gal."

"Don't worry, Mrs. Martinez, I'll take care of her. Thank you for coming tonight, I know it means a lot to my wife." Stein entwined Kerry's fingers with his.

Mrs. Martinez smiled a charming, half-tilted grin, tapped Stein on the arm and then merged into a group close to them.

"I'm leaking like a busted faucet," Kerry said. Stein handed her a handkerchief, and she dabbed at her eyes.

"As long as they are tears of happiness, I don't mind." He turned her into him. She dropped her cloth onto a table and wrapped her good arm around his shoulders. They swayed to the music.

"Do you know what the name of this song is?" he asked.

She instantly thought of his query several nights before, when he asked about Barry Manilow. "I think its "Come Away with Me" by Norah Jones."

"I like it." He nuzzled the top of her head.

"So do I." She sighed and rested her cheek against his shoulder.

The song ended and Ian's voice came over the speaker system. "Ladies and gents, I'm Ian Johnston, the best man. I want to thank all of you for coming to this grand occasion. The last song for the night will be in honor of the bride and groom, some of you may recognize it. Barry Manilow's "Somewhere in the Night." Let's give the couple well wishes and join them in the last dance."

"There wasn't supposed to be dancing. The strings were for background music," Jessica's screech came through the speakers.

"Shh, you're being heard all over the Secret Garden," Ian said, his Irish accent more pronounced than Kerry had ever heard.

A sound like crinkled clothing and hands

touching the microphone hummed through the speakers. The strings played louder. One of the guests stepped up to the mike and sang the lyrics.

"Do you think they'll get together?" Stein whispered into her ear, ending with a slight brush setting her pearl earring to swing.

"More than likely, opposites do attract," she said, and moved with him. She embraced the words of the song and his body touching hers. His closeness ignited the fire, the flames of arousal. The sip of champagne earlier had relaxed her. Her body throbbed. She tingled, though not because of the wine.

The song ended and they slowly made their way to the exit. Kerry stopped to get her purse and bouquet off of a table. They accepted congratulations along the way out of the Secret Garden. Cameron opened the door, and she slid onto the seat.

"I'm going to take you back to the hotel and come back to get Jessica and Ian, unless you have another destination in mind?" Cameron asked.

"No, thank you, Cameron, the hotel will be fine." Stein slipped in beside Kerry.

The privacy shield went up. They were alone.

Stein caressed her arm, stroked his fingers down to the top of her thigh. "Now, Mrs. Laxdale, we'll begin the honeymoon."

Chapter Fifteen

On the way to their room, Kerry clenched her bouquet. The petals flattened against her little purse, while she tried to keep her hands off of him. She stared as he prolonged the removal of his tie, pulling it down bit by bit like an authentic Chippendale, and then freed the first three buttons of his light blue shirt. His tanned skin sprinkled with blond curls of chest hair teased her. The lights flickered on and off as the elevator slowed to stop; reminding her of the last time he'd kissed her in a dark elevator. Her control weakened.

No, don't touch him, because you won't be able to stop. Have some sense of decorum. Something deep inside her urged her on. She was straight-up to distraction, lusting for her husband.

She stepped closer to him, slipped another button from its anchor and slid her hand inside his shirt to caress his beautiful golden skin. Their gazes met and held. His eyes glazed over with desire, or was it a reflection of hers? Kerry elevated onto her tiptoes and locked her lips onto his with a ferocity that didn't compare to what she had experienced earlier at the gazebo under the stars.

The elevator doors slid open. A muted cough broke them apart. Kerry lowered her heels and glanced at the person who joined them. The man gave her a sly look.

"Just married," she said, and wiggled the fingers on her left hand. The yellow diamonds twinkled brilliantly in the overhead lights.

"Congratulations," he said as he turned to face the front.

Stein chuckled. His tight stomach moved up and down under her hand. Fortunately, the sounds never left his mouth. That would have been too much. She twisted around, so her back was to his front, and leaned against him. His excitement obvious as his penis grew hard and large, generating a heat that melted her core and made her ache with a new found need.

She kept her eyes focused on the elevator buttons, the flashing lights indicating its progress. Two more floors and she'd be able to do all the naughty things she'd envisioned in the past few hours, some of which Jessica planted there. Two more floors and a quick flight down the hall. A few seconds and she'd experience the rapture of being in Stein's arms. Her pulse palpitated in her throat. She inhaled and craned her neck to gaze upon the face of her beloved. A soft swish and the doors opened. A slight blush was visible on the stranger's pale countenance, he nodded and turned away.

"Good night," she said. Stein released her hand and wrapped his arm around her shoulder. They strolled down the hallway.

The elevator cables squeaked as the doors closed and the car moved. The metal grinding against metal vibrated off the hallway walls. Eyes locked. She smiled and he chuckled, a sexy effervescent sound. He dropped his arm and withdrew the keycard from his jacket pocket. He slid it through the slot and a whoosh later, paradise awaited.

Warm, muscular hands lifted her from behind as she stepped near the open door.

"It's a tradition. The husband carries his wife over the threshold the first time." He breathed huskily in her ear and lifted her.

"I like it. You can carry me all the way to

satisfaction."

At his guffaw, she chuckled. He was making the night all the more fun. What an amazing day it had turned out to be, beginning with the early morning sex, then the letter and summons. The surprise wedding location and now he held her in his arms. He cuddled her close. He touched her as no other man ever had before, like a virtual arrow straight through her motherboard.

"Put me down. I need to change out of this dress," she whispered and followed it with a quick tongue flick to his earlobe.

He placed his hand at the back of her head, his lips a hairsbreadth away from hers. "I agree with removing the dress, but do you really need to put clothing on?"

He lowered her body until her feet touched the floor. She kicked off her heels, reducing her height to his chest level.

"Tradition." She grinned and gave him a quick peck on the lips. "Besides, I think you'll like the tiny bit of clothing I'm going to put on."

She walked to the table and booted up the laptop.

"Here," she clicked on a drop down box from the internet explorer bookmarks. "Frederick's of Hollywood. Peruse the site while you wait. It'll be worth it." Kerry licked her lips and turned around, so he could unzip her dress.

In a flash, the dress fell off her shoulders. She held it with her hand, and looked back provocatively to see him paying particular attention to her backside.

He winked at her. "Hurry up now, love, I'll miss you."

She grinned like a loon, and he swiveled around to face the computer. His strong fingers scrolled down the snapshots of bustiers. Soon, they'd be scrolling over her. She skittered into the powder room with nervous excitement.

Her white teddy, simple and elegant, hung from the towel holder. She softly closed the door and stepped out of the dress. She placed it on a padded white hanger and looked at herself in the mirror. Could the woman with desire-laden eyes and soft smile be Kerry McClure?

No, in the reflection of the mirror stood a woman in love, a woman CEO, a woman named Kerry Laxdale. She pulled the pins out of her hair and shook it out. She used a cotton swab and make-up remover to scrub her face and gently removed the tint from her neck burn. She wanted to go to him clean and clear of any falsity. Their wedding night had to be perfect. In pleasing him she'd find if he could come to love her.

Kerry washed her hands to remove the oils prior to putting on the sexy nightwear. The soap slid over her fingers and under the gold wedding band. The ring slipped off and fell into the sink.

Her heart stopped.

No!

The ring twirled around and around. She reached down and snatched the circle of gold before it wedged under the metal stopper.

She held the symbol of commitment and love against her pounding heart.

Thank you.

As she twirled the bit of gold in her fingers, she noticed the inscription.

'Kerry, my love. Forever, Stein.'

Her breath caught in her throat.

She sat down on the toilet lid and rocked back and forth. Their relationship had become a fairy tale romance, just like her parents.

He loved her. Why hadn't he told her?

Maybe he'd tell her tonight? He wanted the

proclamation to be a special time.

Kerry had been blessed. She loved him and he loved her.

"Are you done in there? I'm ready out here. You shouldn't have shown me that site. Now, we're not goin' to have a lot of foreplay. I need you, Kerry."

A soft thud sounded on the door.

She rose from the seat, slid the golden band back on her finger— a direct line to her heart. Unsnapping the strapless bra, she removed her hose, and opened the door.

A hiss came from his lips.

She waited for him to move his gaze back up to her face. Their glances met.

Say something.

"I like your wedding night garment better than Fred's." He wrapped his arms around her and hoisted her so her front connected with his naked body and extended penis. Her breasts fit snugly against his firm chest.

"We don't need foreplay do we?" she whispered.

She kept her hands on his arms, lifted her legs, and crossed them behind his back. He carried her to their marriage bed and laid her carefully on top of the fresh, soft, cotton sheets.

"Ah, love, I want you so very much."

"And I want you, my love, my life."

He slowly explored her lips. She hungrily kissed him back, tasting champagne.

Cold invaded her lips, leaving her bereft as he moved his mouth to her neck. He suckled her breast, until it peaked and ached with a need. The second breast begged to be treated with like adoration. She let the siren in her call out to him. The throbbing of her clit needed appeasement and only he could provide it.

"I don't know how much more I can take."

"But, I've only just begun, love."

Oh lordy, was she in trouble. But a very delicious kind of trouble. She reached down and clasped her fingers around his hard, pulsing penis. He sucked in his breath. She stroked the tip, liquid pearled. Her hand smoothed over the head, under the ridge, and down to his nest of curls.

His hands feathered down her thigh, continued down to her ankle, touched it lightly and traveled with slow preciseness back up.

He touched.

He tweaked.

He tantalized.

His tongue found her core. She moaned and twisted the covers with her fingers.

"What are you doing?" She panted. His mouth poised at her secret entrance. His tongue flicked her clit until she wanted more, seeking something. Fulfillment?

"I'm making love to my wife," he said.

She writhed, fighting the explosion she felt near the edge. Stein elevated her into a world, fantastic and new, using his masterful fingers, teasing tongue, and soft lips.

Needing him to fill her, she lifted her hips off the bed.

Chapter Sixteen

Kerry quickened her stride and her breath came out in pants. Her fate would be determined by the people sitting at a round table waiting on her. The sense of banishment overwhelmed her.

If it wasn't for the man silently keeping pace with her, she would not have had the confidence to proceed as she knew she must.

She unlocked the door to her office and breathed a sigh of relief as she entered. The soft butter cream walls and wood floors created a sense of comfort and safety. She stood stock-still, and inhaled and exhaled.

"Don't let your fears drag you down, love," he said as he closed the door behind them. "Have faith."

She smelled the citrus soap scent as he rested his cheek against the side of her head.

"I just don't want to be blackballed by my father's peers." She eased out of his embrace and walked over to the tall windows. The woods were filled with a variety of pines—spruce, white, and Aspen—and beyond the pines were oak, maple and birch. Stalwart sturdy wood surrounded her, she wouldn't bend. She'd remain steadfast like the mighty oak. Mike could blow chunks of wood, because she wasn't going to lose. It was her legacy, her right to take control of McClure Ventures and she would.

She straightened the brooch on the white blouse at the groove of her neck, tugged at the hem of her jacket, and smoothed her skirt. A quick check of her heels proved to be free of smudges. She wanted her appearance to be perfect when she walked into that board room.

Stein's footsteps resounded on the wood plank floor. He slid his arms around her waist and eased her back against his chest. Just having his fingers press low on her stomach sent quivers prickling over her skin, and lower, her muscles contracted. She remembered the things he did to her, for her, last night. The next instant, she experienced a miniature orgasm, the muscles contracting and sending the tingling upward.

"I've always tried to do the right thing, to be an honest and successful leader. My father taught me the ins and outs of business and politics, but I didn't count on this. I seriously don't believe he anticipated the underhanded way Uncle Mike would try to remove me from the CEO position."

"I don't know the players involved, but my opinion is you should go in with a strong sense of self. There's an Irish saying, 'You've got to do your own growing, no matter how tall your grandfather was.'"

He turned her into him and lifted her chin.

Her parents had to be smiling down on her, thankful she found someone so supportive. Stein loved her. She had been blessed to have found him.

"You couldn't have gotten the company this far in the last six months if you didn't have good business judgment. Jessica said The Garden Center has doubled the income in the past month. You're doing a wonderful job of growing."

"I thank you a thousand times, my love."

"Kerry, you don't need to defend your actions regarding me and Rune Technologies. I've known this from the moment I suggested you marry me. They'll keep you as CEO because you're their future. You'll take them into the new age and make their heads spin with the benefits, the profits."

He kissed her lightly. "I love you, so I used the board and their threats agin' you to convince you to marry me. You are my secret garden, a place I couldn't live without."

Her head dizzied and her heart thumped with a steady beat at his words. He said the words aloud. He'd married her because of love. Life had a rhythm, a circle, and she was fortunate enough to have come full circle, desiring something that would give her the opportunity to help others, the business, and to share an unbound love with Stein. "I love you."

She felt his smile as he rubbed his cheek against hers.

"We'll have to decide what to do regarding where we live, Ireland or Indiana," she murmured.

He kissed her lightly as she spoke the words.

"We've plenty of time to discuss it. Ian's flying back to County Kirk tomorrow. I'll be an absentee partner until we settle on locations." He took hold of her hand and pulled her away from the window.

She had a sudden uncomfortable thought about his partner's buyout. Had he been able to conclude the deal and keep his business? "On the subject of partners, what will happen to your woman partner? Will she take the buyout even if it's a few days late?"

Stein leaned against the desk and pulled her between his legs.

"It won't be late. I delivered the agreement to Jeff before we left for Las Vegas. She'll get her blood money, and Ian and I will be free to build our business."

"Speaking of Ian, Jessica certainly has come out of her shy shell around him."

He chuckled. "I never really witnessed a shy Jessica. Do you have any video clips of when she was shy to prove it?"

The door opened and the woman herself stuck

her head around the corner. "Kerry, they're ready for you."

"Thanks, I'll be right there." When the door shut, she touched his arm. "What about having sex with a prospective vendor? A taboo that I'll have to explain."

"Not if the prospective vendor was also your fiancé." Stein led her out the door and down the hallway to where Jessica stood in front of a conference room. "Go in there and be the fierce warrior I married."

"Come with me." She held the door open, beyond in the conference room the members were gathered with ties knotted close to their throats. Old and young hands rested on the table top, ready to make declarations predicting her future. She eased it close, shutting out the men.

"Love, I'd do almost anything for you, but this you'll have to do yourself," he said softly as he urged her forward. "I'll be right here."

She nodded and swallowed, a gurgle erupted in her throat.

Stein sat on a barrel back chair outside the conference room. He listened, but didn't hear shouting, nor did he hear her voice. So intent on Kerry, he hadn't heard the husky, female-voice until the screech pierced his eardrums.

"May I help you, sir?" A short gray-haired woman in a purple business suit settled behind the reception desk. Kind brown eyes evaluated him from behind glasses that matched her outfit.

"No, thank you, I'm waiting for Kerry." He nodded toward the conference room.

"May I get you a cup of coffee while you wait?"

"I wouldn't be opposed to a bottle of water, if you have one." He smiled, and she grinned in return. When she left, he pulled out his cell phone and texted Ian. If needed, he'd write a letter from his company in support of Kerry. He hoped it wouldn't come to defending her to her own people. The board had to be astute enough to recognize her ability to lead and her value.

"Here you are, sir." The woman handed him bottle of Evian. "My name is Mildred, if you should need anything."

"Thank you, Mildred, I'm Stein Laxdale." He appreciated the efficiency of Kerry's staff and the atmosphere. The office was contemporary in setting, with the light greens and brown creating a relaxing environment. The arrangement was similar to his office although his held residence in a monastery back in Ireland.

"Kerry's husband?" Her eyes widened and a smile formed on her face. She settled behind the simple contemporary desk again.

"Yes, I see news travels fast in the Midwest."

"News like Kerry getting married will be sprayed, like fertilizer from a crop duster, throughout several states." She had a small smirk on her face, and her eyes glittered with laughter.

"May I ask why?"

Mildred turned her attention back to her computer screen, but a little smile formed on her aging round face like she held onto a delicious secret. "Certainly you may, but I'm not tellin' you. Ask Kerry when you talk to her next."

****

"Gentlemen, it's a pleasure to attend this meeting. I have to tell you I'm rather surprised you want to award me the CEO position so early. I had an impressive presentation formed. The numbers are extraordinary. Marketing's working on a schematic to illustrate."

"Excuse me for interrupting, Kerry, but this meeting wasn't called in order to appoint you as CEO," Mike said.

Kerry's heart fluttered. Her moist palms slid down her side. She looked at the men at the table.

Michael McClure, her uncle, remained stiff, his red tie knotted around his throat made his face seem puffy and pink. Dom Catlinni her father's very first partner and her favorite of all the board members sat next to him. A silver, bushy eyebrow moved as he winked at her, which made her sweat glands recede a little. Stephan Daniels, Mitch Bordens, similar in statue with beak-like noses presently focused on the papers placed in front of them. Board member Jeff shuffled around in his seat. Jessica glanced up from her keyboard and grinned.

Kerry remained standing. "Then tell me Mike, why has this meeting been called?" She placed her hands flat on the light oak table and leaned forward.

"Your conduct," he retorted.

"Excuse me?" She straightened.

"It has come to our attention..." Mike paused when someone coughed. "...someone brought it to my attention that you obtained a business transaction by trading favors." His pink face flamed. "This conduct isn't acceptable for the CEO of McClure Ventures. This meeting was called to determine if you should step down and not be appointed as permanent CEO." He inserted an index finger inside his collar.

At first anger made her stomach rebel and her throat choke as the pressure rose higher. Then she directed her stare into his beady eyes. He was a weak man. There wasn't any way the board would approve him as CEO, so he thought to move in by pushing her out of the running. The knot left her throat. She lifted her hands off the desk and prepared to fight. She refused to give way.

She shifted her glance to her right, ready to address each board member.

"Kerry, tell us about this Stein Laxdale." Dom

tapped his pen against the water glass.

"Stein Laxdale is co-owner of Rune Technologies. I contacted his Ireland based company six months ago to evaluate McClure Ventures' technology system. My goal is to attempt to connect all of the ventures by one computer networking system. This would enable the timber mills to have instant connection with the paper processing plant. The conservatory to connect with the animal rescue site—"

"Did you exchange sex for a business deal?" Mike shouted.

"Mr. McClure, I'll ask you to mind your manners. Kerry is a lady, and I'll not have her spoken to in this way," Mitch Bordens calmly declared as he narrowed his gaze.

"I don't believe I need to respond to such an accusation, as most of you have known me since I was a youngster coming into the office with Dad." She sat down and crossed her legs.

"Did you trade sex for a contract with Rune Technology? Before you answer I must warn you that we have a witness to your conversation with the owner." His voice held an unmistakable cruel joy as it whipped across the room.

"Mr. McClure, I'll ask you to leave now." Mitch's voice, while low and monotone, brooked no argument.

"No, that's okay. One of the owners of Rune Technology is Stein Laxdale. We've been corresponding for several months and have formed a relationship."

"Ummph," Mike spouted.

"I'll tell you something from my personal life." She paused, twisted the ring on her finger. "Stein and I have fallen in love, and we were married last night in Las Vegas."

Jessica clapped her hands in a silent applause.

"Congratulations!" Murmurs went around the table.

"Jeff, you've met Mr. Laxdale. What is your opinion of his character?" Dom asked.

Jeff glanced at Kerry and then over to Jessica. Would he tell them she dressed as a man and presented herself in a less than dignified professional way?

He cleared his throat. Kerry glanced at Jessica. She looked up from her laptop, an expression of fear in her eyes too. Cripes. The meeting wasn't going to go well.

"I've met Mr. Laxdale on two occasions." Jeff cleared his throat.

Two occasions? When was the second time? Right, Stein delivered the agreement to Jeff.

"He has an excellent business sense. His management style, while somewhat high-handed, is fair and honest. Rune Technology has a solid financial base with a projection of anticipated growth of at least thirty percent over the next twelve months."

"And personal character?" Dom asked.

"Solid guy. Very professional. Nice." Jeff cleared his throat. "Jessica knows him better."

"Seriously, why are all of you talking around me?" Kerry demanded.

"The only thing I want to add is, Kerry loves him, and her parents would approve of him," Jessica said and then focused on her laptop.

Kerry's throat closed off once again, not in anger, but in relief, joy, and love.

"When can we meet this paragon?" Mike asked.

All gazes focused on her.

"Now?" Kerry twisted her wedding band.

The gazes shifted to the door.

"Now would be an excellent idea." Mike's smirk didn't faze her. She would win.

As she opened the door of the conference room, she smelled his clean sandalwood scented cologne mixed with his man scent before he actually looked up to connect gazes. She walked toward him. He rose from the chair and peered inside the room, while reaching for her.

Kerry glanced back to witness the flash of one unhappy expression on her uncle's face. He didn't have any resemblance to her at all. His jowls flapped as he shook his head.

Stein touched her arm. He appeared to be searching her face, looking for answers of questions which had to be racing through his head.

"I'd like to introduce you to the board members of McClure Ventures, if you'd like to meet them?" She pasted on a sunshine-exuberant grin. She tightened her fingers around his wrist and pulled him toward the conference room. *Please let them be nice to him.*

He whispered into her ear. "It's going to work out for you. Good on that." In a louder voice, "Yes, I'd like to meet them."

He tucked her arm to his side. She led him into a room full of strangers, and her angry uncle. She was confident Stein would be well received.

"Gentlemen, I'd like for you to meet my husband, Stein Laxdale. He is also, co-owner of Rune Technologies out of County Kirk, Ireland." She took his hand. "Stein, the distinguished gentlemen before you are the hidden force behind McClure Ventures. Please meet my Uncle Michael McClure, Mr. Dom Catlinni, Mr. Stephan Daniels, Mr. Mitch Bordens, and you've already met Jeff Wanamaker and Jessica Hoke."

"Gentlemen and Jessica, it's my pleasure to meet all of you, I've heard your names mentioned during the past few months. I'm hoping you got the situation all squared away, so I can take my lovely bride on a honeymoon."

"Anxious to be with the little lady." Dom Catlinni chuckled.

Dom was a man who loved life, loved a good woman, and must have seen it in her and Stein's relationship as well. She appreciated the warmth in the tone of his words and the quick smile on his lovely old face.

"Yes, apparently you remember how it feels with the fresh rush of love." Stein wrapped his arm around her waist and tugged her close.

"Looking at the two of you together, yes, I do remember the rush of excitement of being with someone you care about," Dom responded.

"I don't buy it. I think it's a fake marriage, so she can retain her role as CEO," Mike McClure stated.

Blasted man, who did he think he was to insinuate such a thing? Why would he treat her in this way? Michael McClure wasn't a nice person, and it would be difficult for her to see him in anything other than in a disrespectful way in the future.

Kerry crossed her arm across her waist, her muscles taut, and her relaxed stance straightened. Stein tightened his hold on her. She stifled her response.

"Sir, you have insulted my wife and I don't take that lightly. If you need validation of our union, I have documentation. If you have personal issues, I'd like to talk to you in private, not in a business forum," Stein stated. She could feel the rage that begged to be released filter through his hand at her waist.

"Stein's right, Mike. We all know Kerry, she'd never fake anything. However, your statement does clue us in to your business and personal ethics," Mitch declared, his voice dark and edgy.

Some of the members shifted in their seats.

Jessica shut down her computer and shot Mike a fierce frown. Kerry stepped side to side and released a deep breath.

"I don't have to sit here and listen to this," Mike said, his protruding Adam's apple rising and falling beneath his too tight collar.

"No, you don't Uncle Mike. As a matter of fact why don't you forego all board meetings from here on? Jessica will make sure you receive the minutes and continue to get your shares posted. And as a result of my leadership, you can count on them being significantly higher in the future." Her voice sounded calm and controlled, but standing so close to Stein he had to hear her catching little breaths. She pushed her shoe up against his in a comforting and a supportive connection. What was to come?

"You can't prohibit me from coming to the meetings," he bellowed. "You're not CEO."

"Yes, as CEO she can, and all of us will support her. Do I hear a yea?" Dom asked.

"Yea!" The simultaneous reply reverberated in the room.

Kerry stood straight, with a poker-faced expression. Stein released his hand from around her waist as she bent forward and rested her hands on the table top.

"See you at Christmas, Uncle Mike." She nodded toward the door.

The red-faced man rose from his chair so quickly it fell with a vibrating thud. Michael McClure brushed past them and walked out the door.

"The holidays might be challenging if you have more relatives of this ilk," he whispered into her ear.

"Not as bad as Uncle Mike, I promise."

"Whatever, I'll support you and stand by you regardless of how many dreadful holidays are in front of me." He kissed her softly on the side of her face.

The remaining board members stood, preparing to leave. They murmured apologies to Kerry, regretting the meeting had been called.

"When's the wedding reception, I'd like Amelia to meet your young man?" Dom asked. "Amelia's my daughter, Stein, unmarried if you have brothers."

Stein took Kerry's cold hand into his. She tried to control the trembling. "We haven't discussed it at great length. We'll find a date in the near future."

"Kerry will let us know. Nice to meet you, and congratulations on choosing our gal here. She's very special to all of us," Dom said as he shook Stein's hand with a great deal of force before walking out the door.

The other men followed in his wake.

"Way to kick butt, girlfriend," Jessica said. She winked at Stein and left them alone.

"Whew, I'm glad that's over," Kerry said.

"You were brilliant, my love." Stein pulled her close, taking care not to jar her tender shoulder. "I have to wonder, why everyone you know seems to be amazed you got married. I have to admit I questioned if my nationality had provided the reason. Perhaps you had a local guy who they expected you to marry?"

"Until three years ago, I followed the path of God—as a nun."

He loosened the top button of his shirt and took a step back. "A nun?"

"Yep, a nun." Kerry gave him a half-smile. His questioning gaze made her heart jerk to a stop. She realized he needed reassurance. It would take time for them to get to know each other. She'd take the time, because he was golden.

"I'm thankful you changed your mind." He wrapped his arms around her and nuzzled her neck. "I love you, Kerry."

"I love you too, dear husband."